I0669386

MYSTERY MEN
(& WOMEN)

VOLUME NINE

Airship 27 Productions

™

Mystery Men (& Women) Volume Nine
"The Exile From Avalon" ©2023 Jaime Ramos
"Photo Finished" ©2023 Jonathan W. Sweet
"The Devil Takes a Bride" ©2023 Mark Allen Vann
"The Zig-Zag Man" ©2023 Jarrett Mazza

An Airship 27 Production
www.airship27.com
www.airship27hangar.com

Cover and interior illustrations ©2023 Rob Davis

Editor: Ron Fortier
Associate Editor: Gordon Dymowski
Marketing and promotion: Michael Vance
Production designer Rob Davis.

ISBN: 978-1-953589-55-2

Printed in the United States of America

10 9 8 7 6 5 4 3 2 1

MYSTERY MEN
(& WOMEN) VOLUME 9
-TABLE OF CONTENTS-

THE EXILE FROM AVALON..5
By Jaime Ramos

Ex-super cop Frank Steelgrave faces an old foe from his haunted past in the dying city of Detroit.

PHOTO FINISHED...37
(Black Wraith)
By Jonathan W. Sweet

When a prominent female U.S. Senator is blackmailed for past indiscretions, private eye Charlie Cook takes the case unaware it will take the Black Wraith to solve it.

THE DEVIL TAKES A BRIDE..77
(Killdevil)
By Mark Allen Vann

Stephen Kildare attempts to save the wife of a mob killer who wants her dead. Meanwhile, he is still under the watchful eye of his boss; the guy with horns.

THE ZIG-ZAG MAN..119
By Jarrett Mazza

Imbued with enhanced athletic abilities that allow him to move a lightning speeds, Arnold Zigler assumes the persona of The Zig Zag man; a thief no one can catch. But when he is recruited by the mysterious gang boss called No Face, things become deadly.

THE EXILE FROM AVALON
By Jaime Ramos

D etroit hadn't slept in ten years.

It's easy to remember the time before, the time when people didn't fear the water and the earth. Remembering the good times didn't change the reality of today. The people in Detroit didn't believe in heroes, and they were served burnt reminders from the hands of twenty-one ghosts who called from watery graves. The water and the smoke were black and full of fury. A hero would have saved the people. A real hero anyway.

Frank listened to his wife and stayed silent, all the while rubbing his eyes. He sat across from her at the kitchen table and he listened to every word. He stared at her unblinking and motionless. *She doesn't trust you.* The voice pushed its way into his mind. The voice that kept Frank Steelgrave strong and focused. He called the voice simply Steelgrave. When he was in the hospital the doctors had other labels for the voice but he didn't listen to them anyhow.

"There is no way that I'm going back to living that way Frank," Madelyn was clear on the matter and he needed to understand that. The last twenty years had been hell on her as well. Sometimes he wondered if she didn't need a doctor as well.

Frank put his big hand on his wife's hand and asked, "Why don't you believe me?" It hurt Frank's sensibilities and drew the wind out of him. *Did she think he was a liar?*

Frank sat listening and staring at his very beautiful wife. She had classic straight brown hair and a full smile, when she chose to use it. He felt the old hurt well inside of him. You wouldn't think that a big, strong man, a man made of granite, could have so much doubt and self-loathing.

"You didn't see anything Frank," Madelyn sighed and gave Frank a frown, "Are you off your meds again?"

Frank turned his head and looked down at the black and white checkered floor and noticed that the cleaning lady had mopped and polished the floor today. It was shiny and clean and inviting. Sometimes he was so tired, he wanted to just lie on the floor forever. He just wanted to sink into the floor and rest. It looked cool and flat and ...his wife Madelyn was talking again.

"Frank," Madelyn grabbed his chin and turned his head so she could look him in the eyes, "I know you think you saw something, but there is nothing there. I didn't see anything and I don't think you did either." He frowned and she ran her hand through his hair and over his receding hairline. "I want you to take the day off tomorrow and go see your doctor if possible."

Steelgrave swam to the surface of Frank's mind. *That sounds great!* Steelgrave had a lot he wanted to share with the doctor and none of it good. Dr. Lane is exactly what we need Frankie-boy! *I can't wait to see the doctor's cold eyes and hear her condescending platitudes.* Spending time with the shrink always made his day.

"I know what I thought I saw Maddie," Frank was beginning to get confused. Sometimes the *Steelgrave* voice muddied the water.

"Frank Steelgrave, I love you," she smiled simply at him, "But you need to trust me. There is no one outside my office. You're being completely paranoid." Madelyn stood and moved from the table. She needed to start the dishwasher.

Madelyn could have married any guy she wanted. She was stunning and tall and ambitious. She worked as an attorney for the Recoil-Tech Company and he knew how men looked at her. Frank had been lucky to marry Madelyn, especially in light of what had happened. She had stayed with him regardless of what people said.

He turned his head and looked out of the kitchen window and saw some neighborhood kids playing ball. They were running and yelling in the autumn evening. He admired them. One kid about eleven years old made eye contact through the window at him and grinned. The kid's name was Oliver Johnson. Oliver was innocent and didn't remember the years before the radiation and the poisoning. The city of Detroit was a much different place now. Oliver just saw his buddy Frank getting chewed out by his wife and thought it was funny.

Frank felt passionless and all he could think about was sinking into the kitchen floor and resting there. Sometimes he wanted to rest there forever.

◉◉◉

West of Detroit, the black SUV turned off highway 94 onto a nondescript exit into Waterloo State Recreation Area. The exit was seldom used, and led to a gravel road which wound through the forest. It eventually stopped at a gate bordered by two concrete-reinforced bunkers. A simple green sign with white reflective letters read:

ALL VEHICLES SUBJECT TO SEARCH
DIM LIGHTS
STOP AND PLACE VEHICLE IN PARK
APPLY PARKING BRAKE
ALL OCCUPANTS MUST SHOW HANDS
PREPARE TO SHOW CREDENTIALS

The black tinted windows slid down with a soft whir of their electric motors, and the three men within (all ominously wearing sunglasses) showed their credentials to two guards who stepped out from their respective bunkers. The two guards wore black body armor with pouches containing magazines for their 9mm submachine guns. They looked at, but did not take, the credentials. The shield shaped gold and black patches on their shoulders read, "FBOP Special Unit" beneath a golden American eagle. American Flag patches were on their other shoulder. Radio handsets chirped on their lapels. One guard swept a mirror with a long handle to examine under the vehicle.

"Afternoon, Gentlemen. How many?" a third guard asked, stepping out of the left bunker with a clipboard.

"Two from the FBI, one from the CIA," answered the driver of the SUV.

The third guard was handed the credentials, which he examined individually with a UV light mounted in his pen. He copied the names and badge numbers onto his clipboard, and handed them back. Squinting at the driver, he said, "Be advised, you will not deviate from the gravel road. Once inside the perimeter, you will park in space Three-Bravo. Stand outside your vehicle once parked and await an escort from the facility."

"Roger that," said the driver.

The guard with the mirror gave a thumbs up.

The guard with the clipboard clicked the mic on his shoulder and said, "One SUV, government plates, three personnel inbound for Three-Bravo."

"Roger. Standing by," responded the voice on the other end.

The gate slid open, and a metallic block-plate lowered so that the SUV could pass. Once inside the gate, the three men in the SUV saw another sign:

WELCOME TO AREA 77
US FEDERAL BUREAU OF PRISONS
WATERLOO FEDERAL PENITENTIARY
WARNING: REMAIN ON ROAD TO AVOID LANDMINES

Shortly after parking and stepping out of the SUV, the three were met by more armed guards who checked their identifications again. This time, the guards had a portable slot-reader that beeped with a green light each time an ID was swiped.

The agents surrendered their sidearms and hung green visitor passes around their necks with a large number "4" printed on them. They followed the guards up a concrete staircase, entered another bunker beneath a massive tent of radar-absorbent camouflage netting, stepped through a metal detector, were sniffed at by two German shepherds, and finally stepped into an elevator taking them down into the underground penitentiary. The ride was three and a half minutes down, and their ears popped at about a minute in.

The most famous of the inmates there was a woman named Dr. Nora Van Brandenburg. This prisoner truly frightened the staff with her actions, comments, and general viewpoint on all things. She could apparently expound upon all things evil, whether from literature, film, or even history.

Nora Van Brandenburg smiled when she was led into an interrogation room and faced the three agents, one being the special agent from the CIA. He introduced himself as Special Agent Francis Reilly.

Nora Van Brandenburg listened to the introductions and smoked the cigarette that her cellmate had given her. The Federal Government's toughest female correctional facility hadn't broken the ex-physicist's spirit, or her need for chaos. She lolled her head and stared at these men that began to question her. The bleached-out gray walls of the interrogation room and the hard chairs and bright lights meant nothing to her. She was motivated by true love and the malice that can only be twisted by feeling utterly and truly alone. Years before, she had been the accomplice of Dr. Karpov. She was also a sleeper agent, and had posed as Karpov's wife up until her arrest.

"You told your doctors that you heard him speaking to you," Agent Reilly smiled affably and pushed the ashtray toward the very pretty and surprisingly youthful inmate. He hadn't expected her to be so pretty and vivacious and yet there was something quiet and menacing beneath the eyes. "Did you in fact actually hear his voice? Perhaps he is using some sort of Soviet technology to speak to you..." Agent Reilly smiled again and watched as the young woman smoked her cigarette.

Nora grinned and locked eyes with the Agent. At last she spoke, "My doctors are pigs who dine on the souls of those who can't think for themselves."

"Doctors, yes," said Agent Reilly. He pulled a file from his briefcase, and opened to the first page. "Yes, you have no less than four doctors. That makes a panel, doesn't it? I see they've got you on quite a concoction here—to suppress your metahuman abilities, I'll wager. I see you're up to 1800 milligrams of *Amisulpride* a day! That's—that's quite a lot!" he laughed. "It's not even approved by the FDA! And there's two other medications on here I can't pronounce. Tell me, how's that working for you?"

Nora glared at the back of the folder facing towards her. She wanted to make it burn in Reilly's hands. "I see the world differently now," she responded.

"And how is that, Ms. Van Brandenburg?"

"You all are nothing more than hollow shells. Husks. If only I could squeeze your head in my hands, it would crack like an eggshell," she said, exhaling smoke from her nose. "And no more Agent Reilly." She nodded, adding, "*Pravda*—this is true!"

One of the FBI agents touched Agent Reilly on the shoulder. "I told you this wouldn't go anywhere. She's completely lost it."

Agent Reilly put the folder back into his briefcase abruptly, and withdrew a videocassette. "Can you put this on the monitor there?" he asked a guard, who took it. "Oh, I think she's telling us a great deal. See, she was under a KGB special program, perhaps the last experiment in this unusual training regimen out of the *Kremlyovka* Central Clinic. That's in the suburbs of *Kunsevo*, right?"

Nora nodded.

"Yeah, nice wooded area," said Agent Reilly as if he'd been there. He straightened his tie. "But far from your original home in East Germany, wasn't it? Anyhow, the Soviets invested huge resources into unstrapping latent psychic potential in their subjects. They were going to create a new kind of spy. Mentalists, hypnotists—or in your case, a telekinetic and telepath."

Nora didn't respond. She now appeared as interested as everyone else as to what was on the videotape.

"Did you get there by train? Maybe a truck?" asked Reilly. "Doesn't matter. I know you enough, Nora. I know all about you!"

Nora didn't answer.

The guard wheeled the television closer to the table, and turned it on. The three agents and some of the guards looked intently upon the screen. Their reflections gazed back from the darkened screen.

After a few seconds of static, a simple black field with Russian letters appeared.

A countdown followed, the numbers sweeping away with each clockwise stroke of a grainy, black line. There was a beep, followed by a few seconds of blackness.

The picture suddenly appeared. Almost out of focus, there was a clapperboard with Russian letters and numbers in crude chalk, and it slapped shut with a faint noise. When it was pulled off-camera, there was Nora. She must have been in her early teens.

Wearing a white hospital smock she sat in a chair, hair cut short like a boy's, her hands upon her knees. She wore white slippers on her feet. Electrodes streamed down from her head like a veil. A few feet to her right was a rhesus monkey strapped to a board with what appeared to be a metal plate over its chest. Someone off camera spoke Russian to her, and she smiled and nodded. The monkey blinked its eyes rapidly, baring its teeth nervously.

In the foreground, there was a sort of wooden tripod with a wooden clamp. In the clamp appeared to be a slug of metal.

The same voice off camera counted off in Russian, and Nora's body tensed. Her hands clenched, and her eyes rolled back into her head, showing only whites. A second passed. Somehow, the clamp began to jiggle.

And then it happened in an instant. The slug disappeared from the clamp, there was a puff of smoke upon the metal plate and a few sparks, and the monkey was dead.

The image was black and white, and blood began to flow from the hole in the metal plate like ink. The monkey's head rolled forward, lifeless.

The voice off camera sounded in a congratulating tone. Young Nora opened her eyes, looked over to the monkey and smiled. She looked back at the camera, laughing and clapping her hands.

Agent Reilly paused the tape, freezing young Nora's psychotic laughter in mid-frame. Amid the gasps of the men around him, Reilly's expression contorted to an exaggerated disgust. Shaking his head, he said quietly, "Ms. Van Brandenburg, you have been quite successful in fooling everyone. But you can't fool me, because I've been dealing with the mutants and metahumans and every criminal element your sick boyfriend had a hand in making twenty years ago. You can't fool me," Reilly smiled, nodding to the guard to eject the tape. "You're a mentalist. A telekinetic. That was a steel plate penetrated by a slug of tungsten that you moved with your mind!"

Nora appeared curious, as if there was a question to follow. "I did not have anything personal against the animal, if that is what you're going to ask next," she offered.

"You're a mentalist. A telekinetic."

"Karpov taught you how to penetrate the armor of our American tanks, right?"

"That's what the Special Committee wanted me to learn. But not Karpov. He… he believed there was something greater for me. He called me his little artist!"

"That's Karpov's voice in the tape, is it not?"

"It is."

"And, after your training, but before all these medications, you could hear his thoughts, couldn't you?"

Nora slowly nodded. Her eyes seemed to squint painfully. Her veneer of malice and unspent rage seemed to flicker and fade.

"Couldn't you?" roared Agent Reilly, making Nora tense.

Reilly sat down in his chair. He drew a cigarette from his vest pocket, and slid it across the table to her.

"You miss him, don't you? Karpov?"

She nodded. She was beginning to cry.

"Ten years is a long time. Do you think he'll ever come back for you?"

Nora's hand with the unlit cigarette covered her eyes. Her body shuddered, sobbing. The one thing that hurt her most was the notion of never seeing him again—her teacher, her lover.

Her god.

"Do you think he's going to come back here like Prince Charming, coming to re-awaken the Sleeping Beauty?" Reilly asked. The two agents behind him shared glances at each other, as if Reilly was going beyond professionalism.

But then something happened. Nora changed back again. The knuckles on her hands showed white. Her eyes slowly opened. She was not broken at all.

Nora became cool and vicious as she had been when she had entered the room.

Reilly didn't appear to care. "We have it on good authority that he's back in this country once again. Given that the hard-liners and communist party aren't what they used to be, we think he's been working for the Russian mob for the last few years, and know he's back. Any idea why?"

Nora put the cigarette behind her ear and put both of her hands on the table, "He wouldn't come back to this stupid country." Nora started making circles on the tabletop and smiled again. "But if he did, he is not seeking me." Nora looked the men in their eyes and she knew that they were enraptured now. "If Dr. Karpov came back for anyone, it would be *him*."

Everyone in the room knew who she was alluding to.

"Frank Steelgrave?" asked Reilly. "The cop who almost had him?"

"Yes."

"And why is that?"

"Because that stupid cop stole something from him."

"What did Steelgrave take?"

Nora grinned and for the first time, looked directly into Reilly's eyes. "Me!" She said suddenly, tapping her feet on the tiled floor. There was a pause. "And since he can't come for me. . ."

"Why won't he come for you?"

"Because I had to go through six gates just to get to this room, and I was searched at two of them. They check on me every hour. Plus whatever security there is on the outside—Karpov could never get me out, and he knows that."

Reilly sighed, closing up his briefcase. "Oh, I think he's just crazy enough to try. "Guards, I think it's time to go." Turning to the two FBI agents, he said, "Gentlemen, thank you for escorting me."

The two nodded. To them, this had been nothing more than a fool's errand.

"Good luck, Agent Reilly," Nora crooned as the agents were led out the door. "You'll need it!"

"Shut up!" ordered one of her guards, putting on her handcuffs.

Nora smiled all the way back to her cell, even when they shoved her. She knew something that neither the guards knew nor even the FBI agents knew—Agent Reilly was not Agent Reilly.

As the cell door shut behind her, and her cuffs were removed from the bars, she smiled at the ceiling. Her love had returned, after all these years.

Dr. Karpov had returned.

◎◎◎

An hour and a half later, at the Lucky 7 Motel in Ann Arbor, Michigan, Dr. Karpov stood in front of the bathroom mirror. He was no longer Agent Reilly. His eyebrows slowly slipped up into a higher position, and his cheekbones began to soften. His lips shrank, his chin narrowed. His eyes changed from blue to hazel. All of this was noiseless but extremely uncomfortable.

He changed into a sports jacket, took two aspirin, and slicked back his hair. It had taken him an hour to fully complete his transformation into his next persona. The kitchenette's oven in the motel room hissed gas throughout the process, as did the room next door, where the body of one FBI agent was propped in a chair, the other upon a bed. On the bed in *this room* was the body of the *real* Agent Reilly, who had been dead for two days. Karpov almost began to choke on the gas as he finally hurried and opened the bathroom window, threw down his bags, and jumped out himself. Minutes later, he got into a dead tourist's rental car parked a block away, started the engine, and drove off.

The Motel Fire made the 6 o'clock local news as a breaking story.

◉◉◉

Back in Detroit later that evening, the fire was on the television, filmed live, in progress, from a news helicopter. Madelyn and Frank Steelgrave just had cleaned up after dinner and were both working in the den, ignoring the news report that played quietly before them.

Their home was located in a gated community and constructed of brick and mortar, and most of the brick was covered in ivy that Madelyn faithfully trimmed in summer months. The early Colonial house was big and beautiful, with an iron gate that separated the driveway from the street. Madelyn's job provided them a good and fortunate life. Frank and his wife never worried about paying for healthcare, as did most of the people of Detroit. Frank worked iron for Meehan Ironworks and he was happy to have a decent job in this day and age. Madelyn didn't care if Frank worked or not, they didn't depend on his salary, however Frank seemed more focused when he worked with iron and steel. He liked the way he felt bending iron and helping to rebuild a city that had fallen on hard times. Frank's boss, Evan Milo, was a pill however, and Frank knew that he'd catch hell in the morning, for calling in sick.

As Madelyn sat at her reading station in the den, Frank listened to the nightly news and concentrated on doing push-ups. The den was very Art Deco and the rounded edges were very comforting. Up on the bookshelves, there was a small flat-screen television that Frank always listened too while doing floor exercises. He had lost count on how many he had actually completed, so he decided to keep exercising until it burned. Frank Steelgrave was a tall man, he was muscular and athletic. He had played college hockey, while completing a degree in Law Enforcement. Frank was a defensive specialist and was feared on the ice.

This was always a good time at night for Frank, Maddie was busy working on her brief and he was busy fine-tuning his rippling physique. For a man at age forty-four, Frank still turned heads when he walked down the street. It was very peaceful and serene in the room and then the television news blabbed on about the toxic cleanup on 43rd Avenue. There were fifteen buildings being torn down and radiation was found in and around the pilings. Six workers were sick and in the emergency room.

Frank stood up and stared at the television and felt suddenly sick. "Maddie did you hear this?" It would never end, the radiation, the nightmare, the beating he had taken, the scars...

"Yes dear," Madelyn barely looked up from her paperwork. "The mayor said that clean-up efforts were going great until this afternoon..."

"Six guys Maddie, can you believe this?" Frank was staring deep into the television screen and obsessing over every detail. His muscles coiled and flexed as he lost himself for a moment. "43rd Avenue is like twelve miles from the river-front, I can't believe the radiation spread that far..."

"Honey, turn that television off." Madelyn liked to distract Frank from the news for the most part. "How many push-ups did you do?"

Frank turned the television off but his eyes stared at the screen anyway. "I'm not sure, maybe two-hundred and fifty or so...I can't believe this radiation thing..."

"Frank," Madelyn smiled and put her papers down. She didn't really need to deal with this now, but Frank had been so upset lately. "Tell you what, if you forget the television, and meet me in the bedroom, I'll give you a massage."

Frank quit staring at the television and turned toward his wife. "I thought you were busy with the brief?"

She *was* busy. Madelyn sighed, she needed to work on the brief, but Frank was her biggest priority. He was the one vulnerability that Madelyn had allowed in her life and she cherished him. "Go take a shower and get fresh and I'll meet you there." Frank didn't have to be told twice, and he grinned and left the room. Madelyn smiled, she loved that boyish grin, no matter how much her husband had aged. The brief would have to wait, and she would be stuck working through lunch tomorrow. Madelyn looked up at the huge bookshelves on the walls of the den. She saw her husband's picture at age twenty-one in a Detroit Police Department uniform, he looked handsome and confident and full of life. *I am going to throw that damn television away, one day!* She frowned and stared at the tiny television, *your days are numbered.*

Before Frank showered he stopped at the closet in the spare bedroom.

This was the closet designated for all of his clothes and Frank pulled out his old windbreaker. The windbreaker had raised letters on the back that read, "D.P.D. Special Investigations Unit."

The old pain filtered down through his mind and he thought about him; Doctor Karpov. The Detroit press had labeled Doctor Karpov, the Red Storm. "I don't know why my life went this way..." Frank mumbled and put the windbreaker back into the closet. "First I quit the police force and then we aren't able to conceive a child and here I am in my forties." Frank stared down at his surgically repaired hand. The burn scars were mostly gone; the city had made sure of that. The city had made sure to cover up a lot of things over the years. There were no easy answers and Frank knew that it was easy to find a scapegoat. He had felt invincible; he was a man among boys back in those days. Things were much different and Frank couldn't figure it out.

Much later, in the middle of the night, Madelyn rolled over and found that Frank had left the bed. Their bedroom was tastefully decorated and a bit Spartan, because Madelyn liked order and tidiness. The bed was huge and needed to be, Frank was a very large man and took up a lot of room. Madelyn checked the time, and it was almost 3:00 A.M. She wondered if Frank had woken up and was perhaps watching TV. She slipped on her bathrobe and slippers and moved out into the hallway that led to the upstairs bathroom. The bathroom light was on and the door was open just a crack. Madelyn moved forward to close the door to give Frank some privacy when her eyes peeked in. Frank was sitting on the bathroom floor cross-legged and naked. He held a small razor in his right hand and was moving the blade onto the palm of his left hand. Madelyn was shocked and opened the door completely and stared at her husband. There was blood from his left palm covering his forearm and trickling down to Frank's huge left leg. At first Madelyn thought Frank had cut his wrist or something...

She stepped into the doorway and stared as Frank seemed to be almost asleep with the razor in one hand and the number 21 carved into his left palm. Madelyn thanked God as she realized that there were no wounds on his wrists. She did however screech her husband's name and snatch the razor away from him. "Frank what the hell are you doing?!"

Frank was almost in a trance and she could smell the whiskey from his breath as he gurgled out, "Twenty-one people died Maddie...Twenty-one people, do you remember?"

"Frank, that was almost twenty years ago!" Madelyn bellowed and held back the tears. "Why did you do this to yourself?" Madelyn saw the huge bottle of whiskey in the bath tub now and she began pulling him to his feet.

"I don't know, there should be a memorial or something," Frank stammered and let Madelyn help him to his feet. She was running cold water in the wash basin and Frank stared at the bright, white sink and how his red blood made a whirlpool in the drain. Madelyn was fighting back her outrage and anger as she held her husband. Frank's blood ran down his hand and into the sink and Madelyn held him tight as the tears slowly ran down both of their faces. There were two open bottles of medication and Madelyn wondered if this was an actual suicide attempt. Regardless with Frank's metabolism, it would take a lot more pills than this to kill him.

"I'm sorry Maddie," he blubbered and she saw the crazed look in his eyes again. He whispered, "Twenty-one, Maddie, the guys on the force called me twenty-one."

Madelyn hugged Frank. "I know baby, they were wrong to call you that."

"No one trusts me. No one believes in me." Frank paused and looked into his wife's face and kissed her. "I need you to believe in me Maddie." The tears ran down his face and Frank wondered if he was actually losing his mind. He put both hands over his face and she could hear him whisper, "It wasn't supposed to be this way." It was difficult and painful and Frank had to squeeze away this awful pain, and he had to be hard as iron. He had to be like Steelgrave. *You're weak and stupid Frank*, Steelgrave intoned and almost laughed. *Look at you cry like a baby, she's going to leave you, why would she stick around for this shit?*

Madelyn Steelgrave didn't reply. She just held onto her husband and stared at the blood in the sink. Madelyn loved this man that was so giving and so charitable and so sweet, in his own way. She wondered if she should send him to an institution to get more help. Their lives were surrounded with remnants of Frank's past and Madelyn wanted to leave Detroit and the people that hated her husband. "Frank I'm going to fight for you," She couldn't bear to send him back to any institution. "We're going to get you fixed up, Baby." She promised and she meant it. Madelyn didn't care what the cost would be, or what her family or co-workers said or intimated. She loved Frank Steelgrave, whether he was a hero or an iron-worker or something much different.

◉◉◉

The next morning Frank rose early and called his supervisor at work. His boss, Evan Milo was not amused; he let Frank know that he had better have a good reason for not showing up. Frank sighed and put on his running clothes. He loved to jog the five miles to his shrink's office. Frank liked to wear clothes that made him look like a boxer, sweat paints and shirt. His face was handsome and chiseled, very All-American.

Frank was jogging down the street and saw a group of cabbies standing next to their cars. The cabbies were drinking coffee and smoking cigarettes. It was cold this morning and Frank could see the coffee steaming. He waved to the men, "Morning fellahs." He smiled amiably and continued jogging. The men muttered and ignored Frank, and it bothered Frank that they weren't friendly. He thought he heard one of the cabbies mutter, "Why doesn't that chump move to Chicago?" *Do you remember the last time you told the shrink that you saw him? Steelgrave asked miserably.*

Inside the office of Dr. Mya Lane, Frank sat on the couch reading a news magazine. He was bored and wondering how this session would help his growing concerns. He knew that he had seen him on the train last Wednesday. The Red Storm seemed to be everywhere in Frank's mind lately. *Of course you saw him, Frank,* Steelgrave whispered, *he wants you dead this time and there's nothing you can do about it. Look at you, sitting and waiting for this shrink to give you a hug or something.*

Frank waited, rifling through the magazines in the waiting room. Everywhere he looked, every city and every state in the union was moving forward, and Detroit remained behind, even went backwards. Here, an article was titled, "Another Detroit Cleanup" and showed men in radiation suits with five gallon buckets walking down the river, awash with dead, rotting fish looking up at the gray sky. Another article splashed with red letters, "350 Radioactive Poisonings in Detroit this year—only 12 in Windsor? What gives?" And yet another, "Has Canada got it better?" Which showed a side-to-side photo with a teeming downtown area in Windsor, and a nearly vacant Mall Food Court in Detroit. And on the next glossy page, here was a picture of the California Governor and his wife smiling at a splendid lunch on a beachside veranda, overlooking the blue ocean, beneath the banner, "Come to Los Angeles!" as if they wanted you—especially you, you personally—to go there and eat with them: the melon, the shrimp cocktail, the iced tea with the perfect spiral of lemon peel. "Come to Los Angeles! Here is New Life!" it seemed to say—which would make Detroit the Land of Decline and Death, the land Demeter perpetually made more barren and more cold as she mourned the loss of her daughter, which Hades himself had decided he wasn't going to release anymore. And everywhere he looked, the glossy pages slipping in his hands and tearing at the

...and Detroit remained behind, even went backwards.

bottoms as he slapped them past, Frank could not escape the effects of that fateful battle twenty years ago. *Homes and Gardens* had fashions that incorporated radioactive resistant materials, plus a plastic skirt homeowners could emplace around their gardens. Supposedly it could keep out contaminated water, and yet Steelgrave, pausing to think about it, couldn't imagine how that would work. *Scientific American* sold home test kits for air and water quality. An advertisement in the back of *USA Today* read, "Why take the risk? New Disposable Jeans from Levis!" And everywhere—everywhere—were soaps that guaranteed the best protection against radioactive contamination; kids smiling beneath puffy white afros of Baby Shampoo with B22 Decontaminant, toothpastes with special lights that parents could shine on their children's teeth to reveal the presence of contamination, and suds from a squeeze tube for the hands of a hard-working man, grinning over the engine of his yellow 1970s muscle car. "Get the work done *without* taking any chances! DECON Pro and DECON Pro MAX!" Also in the waiting room was an older, box-shaped TV. The hottest selling energy drink in Detroit was called DEFCON 1. In the advertisement playing in the corner of Steelgrave's eye, kids in urban fashions drank heartily from the Artillery Shell-shaped cans, shouting, "Let's show 'em how we hollah in Detroit!" and then their heads exploded in poorly-rendered computer animated mushroom clouds, shattering the car windows behind them. Apparently their heads would remain intact through this process, and they would begin dancing and smiling again. "DEFCON 1—*HIT IT!*" shouted an angry voice at the conclusion.

And while the rate of radioactivity-related deaths had remained about the same for the last ten years, the people of Detroit did not seem to notice. The murder rate was about the same too, and was still greater than the number of people dying from radioactive poisoning. Drug use was also up, but that might have happened on its own. The big three automakers had already left, the new state prison, meant to bring in new jobs, was left unfinished in the rotting suburbs. The police force was now six-thousand badges less than it used to be. And yet the people born in this hollow city remained, for whatever reason, as if leaving and moving on to Lansing or Chicago or Saint Louis or Milwaukee would be a kind of cowardice, or breach of loyalty to a town that was, decades before, a symbol of progress and success and happiness. Those happy days seemed to breathe like echoes through the empty hallways of the tenement houses, of housing projects with ragged curtains still hanging from the broken windows, through the metal grates of the closed shops, and it seemed whisper, "Don't leave me, and don't leave me. It will all return someday—don't leave me!" But, year after year, fewer and fewer seemed to be listening. It was only the hardest of the masses that seemed to stay, as if the forces of time were at work to sculpt the populace into an indestructible race of men and women, a race of resilience, a race of defiance, in a world that seemed bent on stealing them away, or starving them, or poisoning them.

Dr. Lane entered the room looking nice and tidy. She had to be around fifty, but looked about thirty-five. She was pretty in that clinical and condescending way. She was charming like an antiseptic cloth. She never believed Frank either, but she did it in such an indistinct and professional way that it didn't really bother Frank. It was like how people on the street treated him over the last twenty years, he tried not to take it personally. Sometimes it was hard, like when the cabbies ignored and frowned at him.

"How are you today Frank," she opened and sat on a chair across from the blue-collar worker. He stared passed her and sighed. *C'mon doc can't you do better than that after eight years?*

"I'm seeing him again, Doc." Frank leaned back on the black leather couch and stretched his legs. She would notice his bandages on his hand and she would start asking about it.

Dr. Lane laid her notebook and pen on the table between them and leaned forward listening intently. "Frank? You saw Dr. Karpov again?" The doctor stared at Frank, searching his eyes for a flicker of emotion. He hardly showed emotion for the last few years and she wondered what the emotional response would be once she started lightly probing. Dr. Lane smiled. "What is that bandage on your hand?"

"You don't want to know about that," Frank frowned and stared at the glass table in front of him, "but yeah I saw Karpov again, and I know he's stalking my wife," Frank blurted the sentence out and waited for the shrink's response.

He was surprised by how she responded. "Frank, that's the first time I have ever heard you say the man's name. I'm pleased you're able to say it."

This was getting interesting.

"Can you tell me what's wrong with your hand?"

"No, but if you keep asking, I might show you," Steelgrave answered and met her gaze.

"Can we talk a little about what happened on the actual day you met the Red Storm?" Dr. Lane picked up her notes and began scanning them. "Madelyn called and said you're in crisis," Dr. Lane put the papers down and smiled lightly. "I would like for you to identify what conditions have triggered the emotions that are shaping your current behavior. So let's start from the beginning today."

Ok, Frank thought, and then he said "I never knew why I was stronger and faster than the other cops. I had always been faster and stronger. The doctors all said I was a genetic anomaly." Frank inhaled, should he just state the facts or go into detail? "My partner Ruben called on the day of the incident and it was exactly 9:15 P.M, on a Thursday night. Dr. Karpov had been operating as a sleeper for the K.G.B. He came on the radar after his accomplice, a physicist, Nora Van Brandenburg had been busted for espionage and selling classified U.S. documents to the Soviet Union. Van Brandenburg rolled on Dr. Karpov and she told us all about his status here in Detroit…"

Dr. Lane turned on her portable recording device. It wasn't unusual for her to record their conversations for further review.

Frank paused and switched gears, Dr. Lane had heard all of this already. "So anyway, Dr. Karpov knew he had to make a play to grab Van Brandenburg, who was jailed. He boarded a transit bus and took the people on the bus hostage. No one really knew what he was capable of doing, so I was directed to the site."

Dr. Lane listened and studied Frank and then asked, "Previous to the battle, what were you feeling?"

"I was excited, confident, almost over-eager."

"Why do you say over-eager Frank?"

"I don't know, maybe I was cocky."

Frank winced as he admitted something he had previously held back. He had been cocky. "It was different then, the whole Cold-War thing was going on and I really wanted to take Dr. Karpov down. I was young and stupid."

"Hindsight teaches us various things Frank," Dr. Lane kept her gaze steady.

Frank continued, "I was being briefed about a block away and putting on my windbreaker and I just felt so damn strong and fast and no one thought I could ever lose. There were cameras and press and I guess the world was just different then." Frank took a drink from the water bottle he had brought in his back pack. "I felt alive as I was running down that alley. The bricks were flying by my face; I think someone said I was moving at like seventy miles an hour. I knew I had to board the bus as bullets didn't seem to hurt the Doctor."

Frank was almost smiling. "I could see the reporters and the people behind the police barrier as I hit the door of the transit bus. The whole thing kind of rocked, and I began pounding Dr. Karpov with elbows and punches. You should have seen Dr. Karpov's face as I blasted through that door. It was priceless."

"How did the people on the bus react?"

"Well they were all screaming and crying as I burst in," Frank was a little guarded about the twenty-one civilians on the bus. "Why do you want to know that?" *She's baiting you* Steelgrave informed Frank. *Keep telling her everything and see how she twists it around.*

"I'm just trying to understand all of the perspectives involved, and I didn't mean to distract you Frank. Please proceed with your story."

Frank moved forward slightly and looked down at his feet. "The bus rolled over and over from the impact and down into the river we went. I was fighting with Dr. Karpov as the bus filled with water." Frank felt a lump form in his throat. "I tried pulling away from Karpov. I tried to get the people off the bus. Then Karpov began dumping radiation everywhere." Frank's eyes grew dark and he said, "I tried so hard, but they all drowned."

Dr. Lane had heard this all before, but she knew that the twentieth anniversary of Frank's fight with Dr. Karpov was in a few days and she wanted to know what kind of trigger might push Frank over the brink.

"Karpov got away and everyone on the bus died," he said simply. "The city has been suffering from radiation ever since."

"But you healed because of your remarkable abilities, right?" Dr. Lane watched as Frank kept squeezing his left hand and she thought she saw blood oozing from the bandage there.

Frank realized that he was crying and his head fell into his hands. He cried and no sound passed his lips. How could he cry and no sound come out? It was all so strange. He tried inhaling sharply and then heard that awful irritating sound of his own voice choking as he exhaled. God, the pain in his stomach, it had been so hard in that deep, black water.

"There was this little boy, Tommy Mitchell," Frank struggled with this part as he always did when he repeated the story. "Tommy's mother had died on the bus and afterwards at the mass funeral I held that little boy and the press loved rubbing my nose in it. I was the big hero who failed to save this boy's mom. I was the big hero; right Doc?"

Frank felt the Doctor's hand touch his shoulder. "Frank, I believe you. I believe you saw Karpov, the Red Storm."

Frank grimaced and looked into Dr. Lane's eyes. "What? You do?"

She leaned down over the seated man, "Frank, there are six people who were brought to the hospital last night. This is the kind of trigger that I thought might push your imagination and possibly your paranoia."

She doesn't believe you either, Steelgrave insisted, and caught Frank's attention. *He is out there and we are wasting our time here Frank!*

I know.

This dizzy broad is full of caviar and champagne and couldn't care less about a bus-load of dying citizens.

I know.

Show her your commitment. Show her that you still care about them!

I can't.

Show her!

"Frank I think your hand is bleeding," Dr. Lane pointed again.

Fine.

Frank Steelgrave began unwinding the bandages from his left hand and watched as Dr. Lane drew a breath. He smiled, twisted and angry, "Take a look Doc." The cuts that composed the number twenty-one on Frank's hand had already begun scabbing and the blood and the scabs were grisly.

Dr. Lane gasped in dismay.

The session ended.

◉◉◉

Steelgrave stood outside the psychiatrist's office and watched as five police officers approached. They smiled and held their hands out in a gesture of good intention. Steelgrave was on edge however, he knew that something was up with Dr. Lane and now his paranoia was vindicated. There was no way he would go quietly though. She was working with Dr. Karpov, he just knew it.

Frank saw his partner Ruben however, and greeted him politely, "Hey Ruben, what's going on partner?" Ruben studied his former partner and friend briefly and realized that Frank was still in great shape. The two had barely spoken over the years. Ruben knew that Frank was no dummy but he had to lay the facts out and see the reaction.

Ruben nodded. "Frank you're scaring Madelyn and from what I understand, your doctor thinks you might be at risk. Madelyn says you're suicidal and that you hurt yourself. Is it true Frank? Your Doctor thinks we need to take you in for a twenty-four."

Frank scratched the stubble on his chin and recognized an ambush when he saw it. "That's ridiculous Ruben," Steelgrave focused. "There's no way my wife would say any of that crap." Dr. Lane had called the police thinking that Frank was a threat to hurt himself or someone else. *Yes, someone else,* Steelgrave thought intently. *He had to protect Frank from himself.* "There's no way my wife said any of that shit Ruben, and I resent the fact that you're saying she did."

"Well she did, Frank," Ruben put his hand on his stun-gun. It would take more than that, and then Frank realized that all of the officers had their stun-guns out.

"You still can't trust me right, Ruben?" Steelgrave stopped rubbing his chin and backed away slowly, realizing he was surrounded. There were at least eight or nine uniformed cops with stun-guns circling Steelgrave. Steelgrave estimated at least three or four more flanking him from the bushes. They must have gotten the whole precinct involved. Frank could see many young officers who didn't know him but wanted a crack at him. Frank pulled his gloves on quickly and exhaled slowly. Frank wasn't afraid, but it had been a long time since he actually fought anyone. He exhaled and put his fists up and prepared to strike first.

"I loved you like a brother, Frank," Ruben shot back and pulled his stunner slowly too. "We all did. Now you take it easy and I'll guarantee that you won't get hurt."

I guarantee nothing; Steelgrave hissed in his mind and suddenly lurched forward at Ruben with his arms extended. Steelgrave grabbed the top of a parking meter and ripped it out of the ground like it was cellophane. He didn't really want to hurt Ruben, but he was overwhelmed and outraged and embarrassed that these guys would approach him this way, like a common criminal. The way Ruben seemed to be dragging Madelyn into the conversation really pissed him off.

Frank was stung on all fronts by the needles of the stun guns and a hundred and fifty thousand volts of electricity blasted his muscles and neurons. Normal men could be taken down by one stunner, but these cops were taking no chances. Steelgrave was a giant and they remembered the damage he could inflict.

Wave after wave of stun needles hit Frank and discharged their payload of electricity.

A halo of blue fire was all Steelgrave could see as his body twitched and jumped and he ended up on the side walk gurgling and drooling. Frank felt several charges hit the left side of face and he thought his face caught on fire.

Steelgrave could see his old partner's face looming over him like a blue cloud. He thought he heard Ruben's voice penetrating through the haze, "Hey Twenty-One, you should have listened." The blue fire burned out and Frank Steelgrave was riding a wave of burned flesh and fried nerve endings.

Later, after being cleared by hospital security Madelyn Steelgrave sat down on the stool provided. She picked up the phone and stared at her husband. Frank sat on the other side of the glass and wire meshed window and his forehead was pressed against the glass and his eyes were heavy, but she thought she saw a flicker there.

"Frank, listen to me," Madelyn tried making eye contact; it was so difficult because the left side of her husband's face was burnt purple and black and red. He hadn't looked this bad since that fight, twenty years earlier. "Frank, they can only hold you here for twenty-four hours. They have to release you to me tomorrow at eleven o'clock."

Madelyn watched as Frank tried tilting his head and took one finger and touched the glass window. What had they given him? Was it Frank Thorazine or Haldol? Madelyn couldn't be sure. Frank seemed completely wasted. The bruises and bandages were everywhere and it appeared that Frank could only see from his right eye. Frank would heal up and Madelyn knew this because she had seen him heal from worse injuries. She was going to sue the shit out the Detroit Police Department, though.

She hated seeing her man, her reason for being, and her best friend in the world looking so beaten and forlorn.

Frank was trying to speak into the phone receiver so Madelyn listened closely. "Maddie," Frank gurgled out and spit ran down his lips and chin and then trailed onto the floor, "Maddie…"

"Yes Frank, I can hear you."

"Maddie, Dr. Lane…"

"Yes Frank, I'm listening."

"Dr. Lane is…working…"

"What are you saying Frank?"

"Dr. Lane…is working for Karpov."

What? Madelyn could understand why Frank was angry with Dr. Lane, but now he was clearly transferring his rage and paranoia completely. It hurt Madelyn deeply and she tried hiding the despair that she tried not to let it show. She said, "Frank you've got to quit talking about Dr. Karpov. If you don't, they will never let you leave this place!"

Madelyn watched as Frank now lifted his head and met her gaze fully. He stared at her with his good eye and with his left hand he touched the glass. Tears welled in both of Frank's eyes and he began sobbing. Frank was

Steelgrave was riding a wave of burned flesh and fried nerve endings

utterly defeated and he put his right hand over his mouth to stop the sobs. It only made it worse and Frank tried choking it down so he could muster the strength to speak. Frank puked onto the floor and Madelyn was racked with guilt and fear and anger.

Madelyn began to cry too, but she had to make her husband understand, "Frank, listen to me, Karpov has been gone for twenty years. I wouldn't lie to you. You're just upset with Dr. Lane for putting you here. Please listen to me or they will never let you out and we'll never be together again."

Yeah, do you remember how long it took to get out of that hospital Frank?

"No Maddie," Frank sobbed and tried to get control, "please believe me. She is Karpov, somehow she is Karpov!" This was just too much! Frank punched the heavy security glass of the widow with his wrapped left hand and the sound was deafening.

Frank's doctor entered the room with Frank and looked at Madelyn, "you're agitating him!"

No, Steelgrave thought darkly, *you're agitating him.*

Apparently the drugs were wearing off and the Doctor whistled for orderlies to aid him as Madelyn stood up from the other side of the glass and backed away. The Doctor produced a new and wicked-looking syringe.

Steelgrave was standing now and looked directly at his wife for what seemed like an eternity, "Get out of here Madelyn."

He turned and knocked the syringe from the Doctor's hand by back-slapping the Doctor with his right hand. The doctor flew across the tiny room and struck the dark gray wall with a splat. It didn't matter if anyone believed him. Steelgrave was in full control and he would take Dr. Karpov down regardless of what the whole world thought. He would be at war with the entire world if that's what it would take.

The two orderlies burst into the room and each tried to grab Frank and twist him and make him quit fighting.

That would never happen. Steelgrave began grinning. Grabbing him was a real mistake. Steelgrave punched the first orderly in the face and elbowed the other orderly in sternum and everyone in the room heard a sharp, jagged, breaking sound as the second orderly slammed into the desk and it broke.

"Stand back, Madelyn," Steelgrave straightened to his actual six and half feet height and eyed his wife. They were leaving and that was the end of it. As Steelgrave punched down the dividing wall between he and his wife, Madelyn thought, He never calls me Madelyn.

Things were changing.

Steelgrave or the divergent personality that the doctors called Steelgrave was in full control now. He swept Madelyn into his arms. He began kicking in walls knocking hospital staff topsy-turvy.

The drugs had worn off for the most part and Steelgrave had a mad-on. He crushed and broke everything in his way. Soon they were outside in the parking lot. The cops would be there soon, so without hesitation he sprinted toward home and freedom.

◎◎◎

Later, Frank stood in his bathroom, off of the foyer and stood naked in front of the huge crystal-like mirror. He stared at the man that looked back at him. They all believed him now, but the question remained, what was *he* going to do about Karpov? *What are you going to do about it?* The voices screamed into his ears and made them hurt and ache. *Twenty-one people lost their lives Frankie-boy! You think you're a hero?*

Frank heard the front door open down the hall. He was sure that his old cop buddies had called Madelyn. No one believed him before, but now they believed, but not in Frank Steelgrave.

The bathroom door opened and Frank stood in front of his wife naked and he turned his head to avoid her disappointment. "What are you doing Frank?" Madelyn turned him to face her. She said slowly, "We are lucky the police aren't here by now. They must be busy tracking Dr. Karpov."

"I'm going to find Dr. Karpov and end this," Frank pulled away from his wife and began dressing. He pulled on a white t-shirt, which read "Meehan Ironworks." He grabbed his gray work-pants and slipped them on. Madelyn grabbed Frank's arm, "They told me everything, Frank," She seemed desperate to make her point and Frank didn't want to listen. "Section Chief Majors from the F.B.I. called me," Madelyn was in the fight for her life as well, "The authorities don't want you to involve yourself!" Madelyn knew that Frank saw this as his big opportunity to be a hero, to change things.

Of course not, maybe they'll throw me into a hospital again.

"I'm sorry, baby," Frank was sorry that he had made his decision without her, "I can't move forward until I put the past behind me." Frank sprinted out the front door of their house and hit the streets using long strides. Madelyn yelled for Frank to stop and quit being foolish, but Steelgrave was taking over now. *This was the moment,* Steelgrave yelled from his soul.

Madelyn would follow him in her Mercedes, but at a discreet distance, Frank knew that Karpov was going to the female corrections facility located at the basin of the Detroit River. The facility housed his girlfriend and accomplice Nora Van Brandenburg. Frank knew Karpov was back in Detroit for her. There was a station house that made the bridge rise over the river. The station house controlled the bridge, which led to the penitentiary. Karpov was here to finish the job too, his programming was probably triggered and in full effect.

Frank looked and saw the bridge operator reading a paper and smoking a cigarette. The bridge was still up and it was 5:15 p.m. The bridge would lower again in forty-five minutes. He scanned the penitentiary grounds and there were no disturbances. Karpov was on this side of the river. He knew that Karpov wouldn't make a move until after dark and it was dusk now. He knew the Russian would cross the bridge at 6:00. But where was Karpov? He looked behind him down the concrete strip on the river's edge and saw two bars and a closed bookstore. The bars were blue-collar and Karpov could hide in there awhile.

"Ok I see what's going on," Frank noticed the police cars pulling up to a tavern called "Trotters," which faced the riverfront. "The cops figured out the location," Frank frowned and began moving toward the police cruisers. He could also see the Feds milling about with their microphones and their radios as well.

"No way, Steelgrave," Detective Sergeant Ruben Gonzalez stepped in front of Frank and tried barring Frank from walking into the tavern. "We've got this under control partner, now go back home to Madelyn and let us take care of this."

"Ruben, I can't let this happen, Red Storm is in there right?"

"I've got orders to arrest you," Frank's ex-partner put his hand on Frank's left arm. "If you try anything stupid here Frank, I'll be forced to lock you up again."

"What is it, Ruben? Is it the fact that Maddie chose me over you?" Frank said and stared at the hand that held him there. *He has always hated us Frank.* Ruben hesitated and saw the intensity in Steelgrave's eyes and he loosened his grip.

With a quick motion Frank moved Ruben out of his way and sprinted past the growing police presence and the news media gathering. Ruben was pushed back so hard, that he slammed into a camera crew and they all fell into a pile of yells and curses. *You're so stupid, Frank*, his mind shouted as he moved toward the tavern door. The tavern front door burst into thousands of micro-shards of wooden violence and Steelgrave entered.

The bar stank of smoke and industrial by-products. Frank realized he hadn't thought this out when he saw the older Dr. Karpov sitting at the bar drinking whiskey. Karpov was graying and the hard lines of his face had faded to wrinkles. He was still as chilling as that day long ago when something inside Frank had died. Frank didn't really know how to approach this so he thought about the river and walked toward Dr. Karpov, The Red Storm. Karpov had a hammer and sickle branded on his forehead.

As Frank approached, it was like the people in the bar gave way to him. Dr. Karpov turned his head infinitesimally, not looking at Steelgrave but looking into Frank's soul. "You...have...returned for the fight with me?" The Red Scare's eyes glowed red in the amber hue of the squalid tavern. "I see you've lost your tennis shoe endorsements."

Frank turned his head and looked at the civilians in the bar, "You all better clear out of here." His voice was like gravel. "This is gonna get ugly." The people were already terrified; they had already recognized the Red Storm. He continued, "Let's go, Doctor." Frank could almost hear the doubts and contempt of the denizens of the bar as they slowly backed out of the way. Some almost seemed to look at him with pity as Frank moved slowly toward Karpov.

The Red Storm moved like a viper and jumped off his bar stool. He hit Steelgrave with a vicious right cross that landed squarely on Steelgrave's iron chin. Steelgrave's mind swam in a sea of red. His head and upper body crashed against the bar and it gave way and splintered. "You are still *so stupid*, eh Frankie?" Karpov taunted him. "Why don't you just listen to the newspapers? The people of this city hate you. They don't want you and they don't need you."

Steelgrave ignored the taunts as Karpov loomed over him, his mind swam like the dark of the river bottom. Frank struck out with a kick that caught Karpov in the mid-section. The wind billowed out of the Red Storm and Frank could smell the acrid, foul stench of Karpov's breath. *I need to take the fight to him now!* Frank scrambled to his feet and threw a short jab that nailed Karpov in the mouth, then the two of them slipped together onto the floor and rolled around for a moment. Frank felt his confidence build up as he rolled on top of Karpov and was squeezing the older man's throat with both steel-corded hands. *Twenty-one lives* lost that night and Frank could hear them calling out in the darkness of the watery grave.

Twenty-one lives lost that night.

"You...must...do...better," Karpov smiled and then planted an elbow into Steelgrave's face. The force of the blow slammed Frank off of his opponent. Both men got to their feet and began swinging wildly at each other.

Steelgrave knew that he was still in peak physical condition, but he feared the radiation that was yet to come from Karpov. One radiation burst and half of the city could end up sick and dying. He had to find a way to end this quick…and send Karpov back to Chernobyl.

POW! Karpov took advantage of Steelgrave's lapse in concentration and hit him with a looping overhand right, and Frank's eyes dimmed. The next punch from the Red Storm caught Frank on the chin and he flew back crashing and breaking tables and chairs. He flew backwards and through the north wall of the establishment. As the wall gave way and Frank could feel the cold outside air. Crunch! Steelgrave slammed hard against something metal and the car's tires deflated and exploded.

"I love this, Steelgrave. I feel so alive!" The Red Storm bellowed and waved his hands in enthusiasm. "Defeating you again and then reuniting with my precious Nora after all these years!" Karpov started moving toward the hole in the wall to pursue Steelgrave; he was clearly enjoying the reunion. Frank didn't know why Karpov had waited twenty years to come back for Nora. Maybe it was as simple as Karpov didn't have the means or perhaps he didn't want to risk incarceration or maybe the Russian government had kept him busy. Frank didn't know or care really; he just wanted to destroy the man that had ruined his life.

Outside the bar, police officers helped Steelgrave get to his feet, even though they had no intention of letting him finish the fight. Too much was at stake and Steelgrave wasn't to be trusted to actually win. Frank wrestled the cops away and pushed himself upright. His right eye was swelling and closing and he thought his nose was broken. Blood streamed down his face. "Leave me alone fellahs, I'm the only hope this town has," Steelgrave said and he brushed past the officers. Truth be told, they really couldn't stop Steelgrave anyway. The news crews had arrived and were reporting live. They were calling this fight "*The Battle of the Mega-powers 2.*"

"This is Dana London reporting live from the basin of the Detroit River," the very famous and beautiful blonde reporter said excitedly into the microphone as her camera man panned from her smiling face to the ring of police. "The rematch that Detroit has been waiting for has erupted here at Trotter's bar, and we at Channel 2 News, have the live coverage of the police and former police investigator Frank Steelgrave's efforts to arrest the criminal at large, Dr. Karpov, The Red Storm."

Frank ignored the excitement and waved for Karpov to step outside of the bar, "Come on Karpov, you don't scare me…" Karpov looked into Frank's eyes and the evil that lived there was revived and the Red Storm burst out of the tavern and charged Frank. "I will destroy you this time!" Karpov screamed and the news cameras caught every nuance and every expression of both fighters. Karpov swung wildly with two over hand rights and caught Frank on the chin and Steelgrave reeled and hit the asphalt.

Steelgrave's mind spun out of control and everything was black for microseconds and again he could hear voices calling. Frank was almost completely out when suddenly he heard one of the policemen whisper in his ear, "Come on kid, knock this bozo out." Frank opened his eyes and he felt many hands pulling him to his feet and then he heard what sounded like the entire city of Detroit yelling and cheering him to get up and finish Karpov. Frank was groggy but the new rush of adrenaline burned through his heart. *They are actually cheering for me.*

Frank moved forward. He saw Karpov swinging at him and the Red Storm's hands were glowing red with radiation. Now Frank understood why people were urging him on. The people were terrified. Frank blocked a blow meant for his left temple and swung with all his might. The right-cross landed and the force of it hit Karpov with the strength of ten men. Boom and the crowd went wild as Karpov spun around and was staggering back toward the river's edge. *This is my chance*; Frank thought and began sprinting toward the Red Storm.

The point of impact was the Red Storm's center torso and Steelgrave tackled Karpov and they both flew up into the air and dropped into the river with a huge splash. Water from the river blew up and back onto the crowd and cameras and police officers. The news crews and photographers ran to the river to take pictures of the two fighting underwater. As Steelgrave began punching Karpov, bursts of light and radiation gave the crews reference points to keep filming. Many months later, one of the photographers would win a Pulitzer Prize for his underwater, radiation fight pictures.

The black water threatened to overwhelm Steelgrave as the Red Storm began choking him. The two fell down and deep into the river. The entire trauma from twenty years before came rushing back to Frank and he punched and smashed at Karpov. Frank would not die here like the other twenty-one victims. The list was long and Frank had memorized every name and every face. Frank elbowed Karpov and broke the chokehold.

The hands of the Red Storm glowed with bright nuclear radiation and Frank was burning as his skin lit on fire. Frank struck the hammer and sickle brand and Frank's hands burned from the radiation that poured out of Karpov's eyes and face. Frank bashed and punched and knew that he was not only fighting for his own life, but for millions of others. He could see Tommy Mitchell's face in his mind as Frank let out all of his anger and fear on Dr. Karpov. Finally the Red Storm's body went limp and lifeless and Frank stared into Dr. Karpov's eyes. The glowing eyes were fading and then went black.

The press and the police and onlookers all stared and cheered as Steelgrave emerged from the black waters of the river. The crowd went wild and broke the police line and embraced Steelgrave. Dana London ran to Frank as he moved through the crowd.

"I'm here with Frank Steelgrave," Dana was feisty and wanted her interview, and a little bit of pushing and shoving didn't bother her, "Steelgrave, it seems like you just defeated the Red Storm, do you have anything to say…"

Madelyn pushed past the reporter and into Frank's arms.

"My name is Twenty-One," Frank interrupted the reporter and stopped and stared into the cameras, "This is for you Tommy Mitchell, wherever you are…"

The exile had finally returned home.

THE END

REDEMPTION VIA FICTION

"The Exile From Avalon" is a story about someone who failed in life. When I wrote the story I was in a dark place and wondering about my life-choices. A lot of my own fears and insecurities went into the main character Frank Steelgrave. Frank had failed an entire city and twenty years later was still haunted by his inability to take down the villain in the story. Sometimes we all feel despondent, sad, and angry at our personal failures.

Second chances and redemption are rarely given to us in life. Frank was given the opportunity to claim redemption and to beat his personal villain and demons. Most of us aren't given these type of chances. We learn from our mistakes and we are scarred and emotionally damaged and we don't understand why.

From a place of darkness it was important to me to write about a fallen hero who was devastated but surviving. A man who would rise from the ashes and take his life back. A man who could heal from some of the very worst that life had thrown at him.

That's what we all want in life. We want to be the hero in our own stories and live our best lives. We want to pull ourselves out of the darkness and step into the light. This is what I've been blessed and able to accomplish.

I hope that you can accomplish this as well. Frank did, and so can you.

◉◉◉

JAIME RAMOS - is an award-winning writer and editor from the state of Missouri. Currently writing a graphic novel, and a debut prose fantasy war novel, Jaime explores issues of war, violence, love and rising above adversity. He is disabled and currently learning to walk with the help of a prosthetic leg. He is also searching for a kidney donor and refuses to give in to his various health problems. Jaime's wife and son are his greatest source of inspiration and he has a very blessed life. He can be reached at jaimeramos5150@yahoo.com or on Facebook.

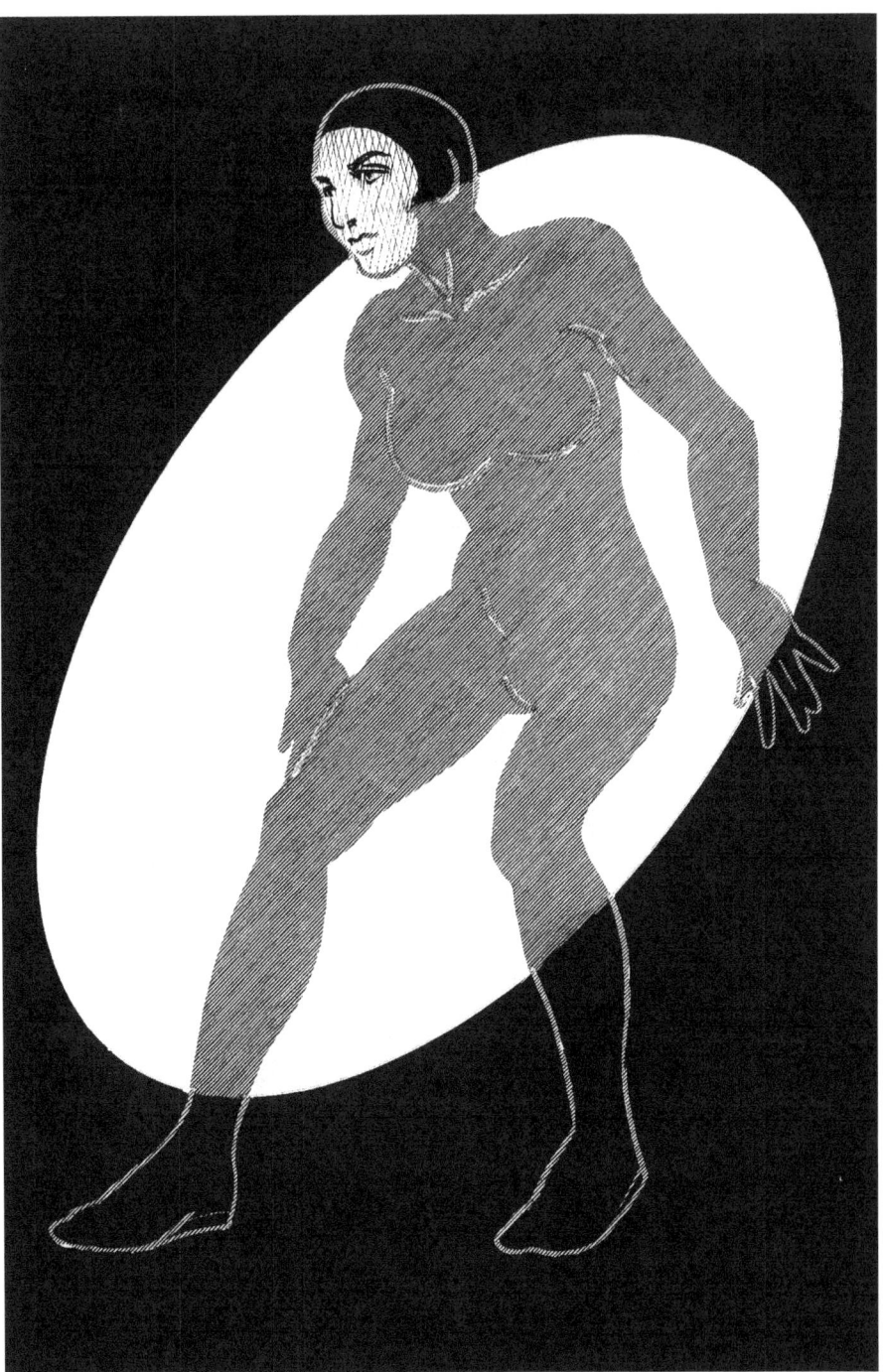

THE BLACK WRAITH: PHOTO FINISHED

By Jonathan W. Sweet

The Café Americano was packed when I walked in, but I found a space at the bar next to a blue-eyed buxom blonde wearing an annoyed look that said she'd been waiting there since Pancho Villa was in charge.

The blonde sipped her martini, gave me the slow-eyed treatment when I offered her a cigarette. Around us was the din of men—and not a few women—trying to close the deal in a mix of Spanish and English.

"You an American?" I asked the blonde.

"And you must be the man from Boston," she responded.

So this was the damsel in distress I'd been sent to meet. I was on vacation in Mexico when Frankie Molinaro sent me a wire and told me to meet up with a dame that he wanted me to help…for some reason. I told Frankie I was on vacation, but when he quoted four times my daily rate, I decided that Sam Springfield, private eye, was back in business.

That all ran through my mind like a shot…like the shot that rang out from the back of the crowded bar before my drink even arrived.

Men started to run; women screamed, but the delightful dish sitting next to me calmly set down her drink and turned to look me.

"Pay my bill, handsome, and meet me at the corner of Hidalgo and Juarez."

Without another word, she eased her way out of the panicked bar. I myself had no interest in speaking to the local authorities, so I threw a stack of pesos down on the bar. I tried to make my own quick egress when a large man—apparently an American—bowled into me, sending me sprawling to the floor. He started pawing me in a way I might have appreciated if it had come from the enticing blonde, but was unwelcome from this overweight, slightly greasy hombre.

"Forget it, gringo, my money's not in any of my jacket pockets." His only response was a punch to the jaw that left me seeing stars for a minute before he jumped up more quickly than I would have thought a man of his size could move.

Panicked tourists and locals continued to pour past me, but I made my way out the door and onto Juarez. Outside I moved fast. My assailant appeared to be long gone, but Hidalgo was just a block away, an easy walk even in the steamy evening air. Rubbing my jaw, I looked for my blonde, but didn't see a sign of her until the voice rang out: "There he is! That's the killer!"

And there she was. Frankie's little blonde troublemaker, putting the pinch on me for the shooting back at the café. I was going to scram, but the local policia were already looking at me, roscoes drawn.

"Do not move, señor," the man who looked to be in charge said as he walked toward me. I was already mentally counting how much money I had left to buy my way out of jail. Innocence had nothing to do with incarceration here, as I well knew. I wasn't sure what the blonde's game was, but somebody was going to owe me big time.

The jefe started patting me down as soon as he got to me and it took him just a few seconds to pull a .38 out of my jacket pocket. *My greasy friend*, I thought.

"Recently fired, señor," he said, bringing the pistol up to his nose.

Across the street, the blonde just smiled at me, then disappeared around the corner.

Charlie Cook threw the pulp down on her desk with a sigh of annoyance. **Amazing Detective Adventures**, *my Aunt Fanny. The only thing "amazing" about this trash is that people read it. Of course, I bought it...*

"Enough of that," she said out loud, jumping up from her desk. She strode across the small office, opened the door and carefully examined the "Charlie Cook, Private Investigator" painted there. *Yep, sign's still on the door.* She stepped out into the hall, looked both directions, half expecting to see a tumbleweed blow across the empty corridor.

It had been a slow month for Charlie—officially, that is. Her nocturnal wanderings as the Black Wraith were keeping her quite busy, thank you very much. Criminals were as active as ever. But paying clients—the kind that made it possible to actually eat and pay rent—had been few and far between.

As one of the few women detectives anywhere near the nation's capital, she usually found herself busy with suspicious wives and other women that had suffered a wrong, real or imagined. A lot of women would prefer not to take their tales of cheating husbands or vanished lovers to a male private eye and that's the way Charlie liked it. But at this point she'd settle for the stereotypical buxom blonde of the pulp detective tale. *Although if we're making fruitless wishes, maybe Douglas Fairbanks will stop by...*

She was thinking all this, lingering outside the office like some desperate salesman. That was when she saw a woman pause at the end of the long corridor—briefly causing a flash of hope—before continuing down the intersecting hallway.

"This is ridiculous," she said, angry at herself for getting so excited at the sight of the woman who was obviously there to visit one of the other offices on the floor. Walking back inside, she decided to send out another series of letters to her too-many clients with outstanding bills requesting payment before calling it a day. She would ignore her own past-due bills littering the battered steel desk for another day.

She grabbed the top bill and started writing another letter to Mrs. Claus. Her husband had been no Santa…but he did have plenty of little helpers. A little redhead, a little brunette, two little blondes…let's just say Connor Claus was firmly ensconced on the naughty list.

Charlie was convinced that, like many women, Mrs. Claus had really hired her to prove her husband wasn't cheating. In her experience, though, once a wife suspected something was going on, it usually was. Either way, the client hadn't been happy with the results of the investigation and had refused to pay. Maybe another strongly worded letter would finally do the trick.

Unfortunately, there was more of the same. She was halfway through the stack when the door opened and Charlie looked up to see the same woman who had passed by some thirty minutes earlier. Seeing her up close, Charlie could now see that although she wouldn't use the term buxom, the blonde woman in front of her was quite young and attractive and, if dressed differently, would be at home in the fevered dreams of a cheap pulp writer. Standing taller than Charlie's 5 foot, 6 inches, she had a cultured, refined look and her clothing told you this was not someone suffering during the Depression.

"Charlie Cook, I assume?" she asked in a strong, confident tone, the voice of someone used to giving orders. "I'll need you to come with me."

Charlie swept the bills and letters into the top center drawer of her desk, then stood up and held her hands out in the universal stop gesture. "Wait a minute, let's just hold on here. Who are you and what is this about?"

The woman, paused, clearly annoyed. "My name is Selena Cleary. I am here to take you to meet my employer. She has a situation to discuss with you and can't afford to be seen visiting a private detective's office."

Charlie, no fan of reluctant clients, offered her own retort. "Listen Miss Cleary. I need some more information before I go traipsing all over town. I'm a busy woman; plenty of cases to work on. I can't just abandon my other clients at the drop of a hat. I have a couple of questions of my own. First, why did I see you walking past half an hour ago and what have you been doing since?"

Cleary's mouth made a surprised "O" shape. "Ahh, I didn't know you had seen me. If you must know, I saw you standing outside the office and thought you might be a client or have a client or some such. There's always the chance someone may recognize me as an employee of Mrs....of my employer. As for what I was doing, if you must know, I left the building and called my employer to try to convince her once again not to hire you. I think bringing you into this is a mistake, but she was quite adamant that a girl detective was the best option for her situation."

Charlie nodded thoughtfully. "Well, at least you're being honest. Now, and most importantly, who is this potential client?"

Cleary shook her head. "No, I'm afraid on that I must be quite adamant. You are not to know her name unless you come with me."

Charlie started to object, but Cleary continued on. "My employer anticipated you might have some objection to that...request. With that in mind, she would like to offer you this retainer as an incentive. Come and see her and whether you take the case or not, the money is yours," she said, handing over a cashier's check.

Charlie was already preparing her response when she looked down at the amount on the check. Some rapid mental calculations told her it was enough to cover all the bills stuffed in her desk drawer, plus get her two months ahead on the rent for her apartment *and* the office.

"What are we waiting for, Miss Cleary? Let's go see this mysterious employer of yours!"

◉◉◉

There had been a driver and black Cadillac sedan waiting at the curb when Charlie and her mysterious visitor arrived on the street. After a few questions prompted only monosyllabic answers, Charlie gave up trying to engage Miss Cleary in conversation and settled back in the luxurious leather seats. For someone who spent most of their time traversing the city on public transportation or by foot, it was a welcome respite.

It was less than fifteen minutes later when they arrived at the Kingery Plaza, a hotel that was patronized by the wealthy and the important in the district. The "residence of the presidents" had seen numerous presidents and vice presidents spend the night there, including the current occupant of the vice presidency, who had spent most of his term in residence. Its central location made it easy to get to the Capitol, White House or other government buildings. That could explain why her potential client didn't want anyone to know she was seeking out a private eye.

Charlie barely had time to enjoy the luxurious lobby, though, as Cleary whisked her past the front desk and right into the elevator. They rode up in silence after they were greeted by the septuagenarian operator. Charlie was admittedly a little disappointed when they stopped at the 12th floor. The vice president, she knew, lived in the penthouse on the 14th floor. Still, you didn't stay at the Kingery without some serious money *and* influence.

The suite may not have been the penthouse, but it was still about three times larger than Charlie's apartment and much nicer than anywhere she'd ever stayed. A glistening chandelier hung over the foyer; deep plush carpets and opulent finishes played out in front of her.

"Please have a seat," Cleary said, gesturing toward the sitting room. "It will just be a minute." She disappeared down the corridor to what Charlie assumed were the bedroom...or bedrooms, more likely.

Like Miss Cleary, the furniture seemed designed more for looks than comfort, so Charlie opted to stand. As she surveyed the room, she noticed the large picture window that overlooked the White House grounds in the distance. At one time it probably would have been considered a majestic view, but the hotel's architects probably hadn't taken the large Hooverville in the nearby park into account. Charlie shuddered as she thought of her own misadventure in one of the homeless encampments earlier that year.

"It's really a shame, isn't it?" said a voice from behind her. Charlie spun around to see her presumed client walking into the room. "People left with no recourse but to live in shacks like that? You would think seeing them there everyday would get the president to do something, but I don't think anything will move that man. Although maybe Roosevelt will move him out in a few months if all goes well."

At first glance, the woman appeared to be as young as her early thirties. A closer look, however, revealed the slightest of wrinkles around the eyes and mouth, pushing Charlie's estimate closer to forty five. There was also something very familiar about her. While not as tall as Miss Cleary they seemed cut from the same cloth. Charlie was sure she had seen her picture somewhere before. In the paper, perhaps the wife of someone important...

The client smiled tightly as she held out her hand. "Please sit, Miss Cook," she said before taking a seat on the small loveseat. Charlie chose a chair directly opposite her. The client lifted a pitcher of ice water from an adjacent table, and poured two glasses.

"Thank you for agreeing to come see me," she began; a grim look on her face.

Charlie smiled briefly. "Your emissary—and your check—were quite convincing, Mrs...."

"Right to it, then? I can appreciate that Miss Cook," she said, her own smile also making a brief appearance. "I thought you might recognize me, to be honest. I don't mean that to sound conceited, but I have been in the papers a lot lately."

"You do look familiar to me, but I tend to find myself a little too busy to read the paper most days."

"Well, then, I suppose that's fair. My name is Margaret Hudson. Ahh, I see you've got it now."

Yes, she certainly had it, Charlie thought. That would be Margaret Hudson, newly minted senator from the great state of New York. Hudson had been appointed by the state's governor to fill the seat of her recently deceased husband, four-term Senator Franklin Hudson, until that fall's election. If Charlie remembered correctly, the new senator was also about forty years younger than her extremely wealthy former husband, something that had not escaped comment by some in the fourth estate.

"Yes, Mrs. Hudson. It's all coming back to me now, but I have to ask, what made you seek me out? I have to imagine that someone in your position has ample resources."

Hudson nodded before continuing. "I've done a little research on you, Miss Cook, and I've been told you have a way of taking care of problems, especially those plaguing women. I've also been told that you can be trusted to exercise the utmost discretion."

She usually heard some variation of this speech when a woman was going to ask her to investigate a philandering husband. But while Charlie had seen plenty of odd cases, a cheating corpse seemed unlikely.

"Of course. Any client can count on me to keep their secrets."

"Even if you don't take the case?"

"Yes, your check makes you a client. Even if we go our separate ways, that confidentiality applies."

Hudson sat up straighter and looked directly at Charlie. "Good. Well, Miss Cook, the short version is that I'm being blackmailed, but let me tell you the longer version."

The senator explained that she was her late husband's second wife, a marriage that had caused some scandal when it had occurred nearly twenty years earlier. The then-twenty-five-year-old Margaret Walsh was a member of a Broadway chorus line when she had met the sixty-six-year-old senator only six months after the death of his first wife. After a whirlwind courtship, they had married, against the advice of almost all his friends and family. The Hudsons were old money, and it had rankled most of his contemporaries that the senator was marrying a woman who had come from "common stock"—and an actress to boot.

"But despite all that, we were happy for almost two decades," she said. "Even most of his family came around, except for his daughter. It was hard at first, but gradually I was, if not welcomed, at least grudgingly accepted as a part of his social class."

She stopped and sighed, seemingly reluctant to continue. She took a long drink of water before going on.

"There are parts of my past that even Franklin didn't know about. I grew up in a small town in Ohio and made my way to New York City with hardly any money. I did some things I'm not proud of; worked in some illegal clubs and spent some time with a rather unsavory group."

"Everyone has skeletons in their closet, but at this point do you really think people will care about you having to take some less-than-legal jobs?"

Hudson shifted in her seat. "There's more. There are...pictures."

"And by 'pictures' you mean..."

"Yes," the senator replied. "Pictures that show me in various states of undress. I was trying to make it as an actress and I met someone who said he could help me get to Broadway. Before I knew it, I was posing in nothing but my undergarments. I honestly thought the pictures had all been destroyed years ago, but clearly that's not the case."

She lifted a small folder off the table and handed it to Charlie.

"These started coming two weeks ago; right after my appointment was announced. There have been three letters so far."

Charlie opened the folder and read the top note.

Dear Mrs. Hudson,

Congratulations on your appointment to the U.S. Senate. One of the first women senators in the country. That is quite an honor. It would be a shame if anything were to sully that honor or the memory of your late, great husband, a fine public servant.

We have come into possession of certain photographs. We're sure you know that of which we speak. We have no desire to embarrass you by making these images public. We merely will need you to do us one little favor and then you will never hear from us again.

Please respond back via the personal ads in the Washington Post with the simple note, "Thanks for the package. See you soon. MH"

"I chose to ignore the first letter, thinking maybe it was a hoax of some kind, but then…" she said, pointing at the folder.

Charlie flipped to the second letter.

Dear Mrs. Hudson,

We were disappointed to receive no response to our first letter, but we understand you may not have realized the seriousness of our missive.

Enclosed you will find an example of the photographs that are in our possession. Please respond immediately as instructed in our first note. Do not force us to do something we will all regret.

"I responded with the ad. The thought of those pictures being public now after all these years…I just couldn't handle it. At the time, I figured all they wanted was money. And honestly, Franklin left me so much money, that my plan was just to pay them and hope they would go away."

Charlie shook her head as she said, not unkindly, "Unfortunately, that's rarely how blackmail works. They usually won't stop until they bleed you dry."

"It turns out that won't be a problem. Read the third letter," the senator said, nodding toward the folder. "It arrived yesterday."

Dear Mrs. Hudson,

Thank you for your prompt reply.

You may be wondering just what is it that we want. We're sure you are expecting an exorbitant amount of money. Let us put your mind at ease. We don't want a single dime from you. We merely want you to do one little thing for us. Next week, Senate Bill 1435 will be coming up for a vote.

Vote "yes" on the bill and you'll never hear from us again. Vote "no" and the photos are released to every reporter in New York and Washington.

We hope you make the right choice.

◉◉◉

Charlie re-read the letters, more slowly this time, looking for patterns in the writing or any other clues to the writers' identity.

"You'll have to forgive me, Senator Hudson. What is Senate Bill 1435?"

The senator grabbed a second folder from the table and passed it to Charlie.

"No apology necessary," she replied. "I didn't know myself when I got the letter. It turns out it would put new restrictions on coal mines; require them to improve working conditions for the miners. There are some rules related to safety, hours worked, that sort of thing. Certainly not my area of expertise."

With the evenly divided Senate, she explained, it looked like the vote would be close. The ninety-six senators were split not by party lines but along more practical ones. Those who represented states with large mining operations tended to favor fewer restrictions, saying it could lead to more job losses in the already depressed economy. At the same time, the growing outcry from workers displaced by the Depression was putting increased power in the hands of progressive candidates in favor of more rights for workers.

"Personally, I'm undecided about the bill," Hudson added. "I grew up around coal miners in Ohio. It's a dirty, dangerous job and they deserve to be protected, but at the same time I know that if we push the mine operators too far, too fast, they'll close up shop. Honestly, this only makes me more likely to vote against it."

The senator wasn't the first to be pressured into a vote, Charlie knew, and she wouldn't be the last. But that didn't mean the detective was inclined to ignore the problem either…especially when it was happening to someone with the financial resources of the widow.

"I can understand that, but are you really willing to accept what could happen if I can't figure out who is behind this?" Charlie asked. "No reputable paper will run the pictures, of course, but they'll report on them and, if I know some of the journalists in town, in lurid detail."

The senator smiled. "That sounds like the advice of someone who is going to 'take the case,' as they say."

Charlie smiled back. "I have to admit you have me intrigued."

"Wonderful. I understand these things can change, but you've probably got less than a week until the vote. I assume this will cover your fees?" she said, handing Charlie a check. A quick glance showed that it was about five times her regular daily rate, even if she worked a full week on the case. *There are advantages to working for the wealthy*, Charlie though, *especially when they pay ahead of time.*

◉◉◉

It was already dark by the time the senator's driver had taken her from the Kingery to her apartment and that suited Charlie's plans for the evening just fine. The driver, on the other hand, seemed quite concerned about

"I have to admit you have me intrigued."

leaving a young woman alone in her neighborhood.

"I know it's a step or ten down from the Kingery, but it's home," she said. "And I can take care of myself, don't worry."

The driver still waited until she had walked inside the building before speeding away, presumably eager to leave while he still had all his hubcaps. One thing that never failed to surprise visitors to the District was how one could go from the ultimate in wealth and luxury to abject poverty in only a few blocks. While there were certainly worse neighborhoods than hers, the simple apartment looked even more drab than usual after spending a couple of hours at the Kingery.

On the other hand, a questionable neighborhood had its benefits. The landlord never came by if the rent was paid promptly and the neighbors kept to themselves, both welcome for someone who took part in what some might consider an unusual lifestyle. Most of the occupants knew that the landlord wasn't going to take care of most repairs, so everyone took it upon themselves to fix or upgrade their own apartments.

Improvements like a little extra security in the form of a double lock and reinforced door frame, hidden storage spaces under the floor and a false back to her closet all helped to make Charlie's double life a little easier.

As she had learned from the senator, the largest and loudest opposition to the bill was coming from a group of coal mine owners calling themselves the American Coal Association. They operated out of an office in the District, not far from the Capitol. While going to see them during the day was certainly an option, Charlie thought a nocturnal visit by the Black Wraith just might provide more information.

Clad in a skin-tight black suit, she examined her reflection in the floor-length mirror and nodded with approval. The suit served many purposes. Its dull black material helped her hide in the dark of night, and also cut down wind resistance. An experiment several years earlier had given her the ability to become, while not invisible, as close as someone could hope for. Combined with the suit, she could for all intents and purposes disappear into the shadows, unnoticed unless she wanted to be. It was a useful talent, but the effort took a lot out of her and she preferred to rely on more conventional means of hiding whenever possible.

And that was its final benefit, she thought with a smile. The skin-tight outfit had allowed her on more than one occasion to easily dispatch a male guard distracted by her appearance. The black mesh mask gave the Black Wraith perfect visibility, but left her identity hidden, certainly an advantage when her cases as Charlie Cook, Private Investigator, overlapped with a project for the Black Wraith.

Even though it was after midnight by the time she made her way the twelve blocks to the Winwood Building where the coal association had its headquarters, she kept to the shadows to avoid prying eyes. It was a pleasant, cool night after the humid day, but she still wouldn't have minded having the senator's driver at her disposal, she thought.

She may not have inherited a large fortune from her late father like some masked avengers, she thought, but at least he had passed on his investigative skills. Forest Cook had been an expert investigator who gave up in a career in the U.S. Navy when his young wife died, leaving him a single parent. He became a private detective who rarely failed to solve a case, right up until his final investigation ended with him being shot in his office. Charlie had been working for her father as long as she could remember, investigating cases in the field before she finished high school. It had seemed the most natural idea to take over the family business.

She paused in the small park across the street from the Winwood Building and looked for any sign of security. No lights on in any of the offices as far as she could see and she noted with some satisfaction that the shine from the lone street light didn't reach the front door.

Although she expected to make short work of the lock, no reason to take any chances. She raced across the street and after a quick look around to be sure she was still unobserved, went to work on the lock. It was a particularly cheap model and she picked it in less than a minute.

I always tell my clients, never cut corners on security, she thought, shaking her head.

There was no sign of life in the building, so the Black Wraith ran up the front stairs to the second-floor headquarters of the association. Another cheap lock, she saw with a smile. She was just about to crouch down to grab the doorknob when she realized she was suddenly warmer. As she felt the heat and smelled the smoke she tried to throw herself to the side, twisting away from the door as it exploded outward. The collision lifted her body and slammed it across the hallway into the opposite wall where she briefly felt the impact before she slid to the floor, unmoving.

◉◉◉

The Black Wraith awoke, coughing, as smoke poured out of the burning offices of the American Coal Association. She had been out for only a few moments, she thought, but it looked like the entire building was going to quickly be engulfed in the fire.

She tried to stand up, but a wave of dizziness pushed her back to her knees. Before she could make a second attempt she felt two powerful arms lifting her up. She reflexively pushed back against the man holding her, sending him sprawling on the floor.

"Jeesh, lady, I'm trying to get you out of here," the man said, grabbing her under her arms again and starting to drag her down the hall. "This whole place is going up."

Her head starting to clear, the Black Wraith got back to her feet, only keeping her balance by leaning against the unknown rescuer. She grabbed hold of his arm and allowed him to lead her out of the burning building. They stumbled down the stairs, the heat and smoke making it difficult to see and breathe. But the man never faltered; his grip on her firm and reassuring.

As they pushed their way through the front door to fresh air, the man finally spoke again.

"You all right?"

The Black Wraith attempted to answer, but only ended up coughing again. Instead, she nodded.

"Don't try to talk. Let's get over there," he said, indicating a bench at the edge of the park. In the distance, she could already hear the approaching sirens. She finally got a first, admittedly blurry, look at her rescuer as he set her down on the park bench. Brown hair, standing about six feet tall, the dark made it difficult to make out too much more. He looked at her with concern in his bespectacled eyes.

"You'll be able to catch your breath easier if we take this off," he said, reaching for her mask.

He let out a cry of surprise as the Black Wraith's hand flew up, stopping his arm in an iron grip.

"OK, then. The mask stays. I'm sure there's a good reason why you were trying to break into the association's office late at night wearing what is admittedly a very attractive costume."

The Black Wraith followed his eyes down and realized for the first time that much of the top half of her outfit had been shredded in the explosion, leaving little to the imagination. She quickly covered the exposed skin with her hands.

"Anyway, it's a story I'd love to hear sometime, but I'd really prefer not to be here when the police and fire department arrive.

"And that," he said, glancing down the street, "appears to be imminent.

Don't worry. They'll take good care of you."

With that, he ran down the street away from the approaching sirens.

The Black Wraith, of course, also had no desire to be found by any of the responding agencies—or to deal with their questions. While her head still throbbed, and her body ached, she was able to warily get to her feet.

She said a silent *thank you* when there was no wave of dizziness this time. She slipped into the darkness of the park and made her way carefully through the open space, thankful for the lack of light.

There's no way I'm making it home dressed like this, she thought. *Not unless I want to get arrested for indecent exposure.*

Just down the street there was, she knew, a 24-hour diner that had a phonebooth. In her line of work, the Black Wraith had made a point of knowing where nearly every late-night business was in the District. Luckily, she saw as she approached, the elderly counterman and his even older lone customer had both come out to see what all the fuss was about. With their attention focused down the street, she was able to slip in the front door and make it to the phonebooth unnoticed.

She had the operator connect her to the number she knew by heart. It only rang twice before a sleepy "Hello?"

"Uncle Kenny? I need a ride," she said, telling him to pick her up down the street.

That taken care of, she let out a loud sigh and opened the door of the phonebooth, stepping out to find both of the elderly night owls staring at her. The counterman dropped the coffee pot he had been carrying, spraying the hot liquid everywhere, narrowly missing his the customer sitting back at the counter.

"Well, darn it, fellas. I was going to ask for a cup of coffee while I waited for my ride. Still, it is a little chilly out there. Either one of you happen to have an extra coat?"

◉◉◉

When Detective Ken Walker showed up fifteen minutes later in his unmarked police sedan, the Black Wraith sprinted from the dark doorway where she had been hiding and leapt into the front seat.

Walker took one look at her and burst into laughter.

"It's not funny, Uncle Kenny," she said, pulling off her mask.

The fifty-year-old Walker, while not actually Charlie's uncle, was the closest thing she had to family after her father's murder. The two men had met serving in the U.S. Navy. Walker had stayed in the Navy up through the Great War and joined the Metropolitan Police Department when he returned stateside. He was one of the few people who knew about her double identity.

"Yeah, it really is," he replied. "You know, your father paid good money for you to go to school and not end up making a living dressed like that."

Her only response this time was a death glare in his direction.

He reached behind his seat and grabbed a shirt. "Here, put this on. It'll be a little big but it will get the job done."

Walker continued driving away from the Winwood Building as she buttoned up the shirt. "I assume you had something to do with that?" he asked, flicking his thumb in the direction of the growing fire.

"I didn't start it if that's what you mean, but I was there when the fire started," she replied, telling him everything that had occurred that day, starting with her meeting with the new senator and continuing up to the fire.

"Do you think your unknown gentleman was the one who started the fire?"

Charlie tilted her head to the right as she thought about that. "I suppose that's possible. Maybe he thought the building would be empty and didn't want anyone to get hurt, so he dragged me out. It would explain why he didn't want to stick around."

Walker turned and looked at her as he pulled up in front of her apartment building. "I would have thought you learned your lesson about getting involved in politics after that mess with the White House this summer."

She raised one eyebrow, a mischievous look in her eyes. "But it was a really big check...did I mention that?"

"I'm serious, Charlie. You know, you're lucky you weren't hurt worse. From what you tell me, you might not have gotten out of there if this guy hadn't been there to get you the street."

"We've been through this. This is what I have to do. I can't just ignore all the suffering out there. I've been given this gift and, well, I have to use it. Plain and simple."

He shook his head as a look of concern played across his face.

"Just be careful."

"When am I anything but?" she said as she stepped out of the car. "Thanks for the ride, Uncle Kenny. I'll bring the shirt back tomorrow."

◉◉◉

It was nearly noon before Charlie made it into the office the next day. It might have been even later if she hadn't been awakened by a pounding on her apartment door at around 10 a.m. It had taken hours to clean up and attempt to repair her outfit—a futile effort in the end. She had multiple costumes, but a hero on a budget needs to make the most of what they have.

"This better be important," she had muttered as she made her way to the door, the pounding on the door alternating with the pounding in her head to make one long painful melody.

"What?" she said as she yanked open the door and saw Detective Walker.

"And good morning to you, too, sunshine. You're the one who woke me up out of a nice restful sleep early this morning, I'll remind you."

"Yeah, yeah," she said, waving her hand at him. "At least tell me you brought breakfast."

"Of course," he replied, holding up a bag. "Cinnamon rolls from Ellie's. I know better than to think you'd have anything to eat here. Any chance you can at least make some coffee?"

"That I can do," Charlie said as she started walking back toward the cramped kitchen, Walker following. "So to what do I owe the pleasure of this early morning visit?"

Walker chuckled. "It's not really that early, Charlie. Like most people, I've already been working for a few hours…which is what brings me here. I thought you might like to know some more about your fire."

Charlie silently gestured for the detective to continue. Walker pulled out a small notebook and started reading from it.

"So the mine owners are blaming the union for the fire—calling it an attempt at shutting down their efforts to oppose that safety bill. The union says they had nothing to do with it, of course.

"Let's see," he said, flipping to the next page in his book. "Two witnesses to the fire, it looks like. Both said they saw two people run away from the fire, but as dark as it was they couldn't provide much in the way of details. One said she saw two men run from the fire; the other said it was definitely a man and a black woman, although he used a different term before launching into a tirade about how 'those animals' were ruining the city. In other words, no one got a good look at you.

"Although you may be interested to know that two well-known drinkers in the neighborhood are telling a story about a nearly topless woman showing up in the 24-hour diner. They seemed very impressed with you."

Charlie looked up from her cup of coffee to offer a wry smile. "I'm so glad to have fans, but the rest of it is good news, I guess."

The two had spent another few minutes discussing the case, but the department had few leads at this point.

Now, as she sat in her office pondering the fire, Charlie was bothered by the coincidence of her arrival only moments before the office was destroyed. And who was that mysterious man? Had he set the fire or was he just another unplanned victim?

The problem was, no one knew that she had been planning on heading there last night. Her client had pointed her in the direction of the association, of course, even if she hadn't known exactly when she would check the group out. The question was what could the senator gain by sending her there only to destroy any possible evidence?

That line of thought was interrupted by the opening of the door to her office.

"Yes, can I…oh, good morning Miss Cleary," she said, recognizing the senator's assistant.

"It's hardly morning, Miss Cook," Cleary sniffed. "Regardless, the senator sent me to get an update from you. She heard about the fire at the association offices last night and is concerned about the publicity. She hopes you will be able to solve this problem quickly."

Charlie made no effort to hide the exasperated note that slipped into her voice. "It's been barely twenty-four hours since the senator hired me. But yes, I'm well aware of the fire. I'm working on the case, don't worry. And I have to say, for someone so worried about attention, having you show up at my office today seems like a bad idea."

Cleary answered with something that sounded like a harrumph before continuing. "Be that as it may, we expect regular updates. You can reach me at this number and I can pass anything on to the senator," she said handing Charlie a small card. "If we don't hear from you, you'll hear from me."

Cleary pivoted and stormed out of the office before Charlie could come up with a reply.

"It's a good thing that was a damn big check," she said under her breath as she heard the sound of the woman's heels clicking down the hall.

She had the letters out on her desk, and re-read them for what had to be at least the tenth time. No clues presented themselves. The senator had also provided the name of the man who originally took the photos, but telegrams to New York had so far proven to be a dead end. She had asked another detective she knew there to look into it rather than take the time to go to the city herself.

At this point, her only other lead appeared to be the fire, so visiting the union leaders seemed to be the most likely next step. The word was that they were using a coffee shop near the burned out Winwood Building as their makeshift headquarters, apparently all the better to keep an eye on the enemy.

The door from the hall suddenly flew open and a new visitor pushed his way in. He was already talking as he strode across the small office to her desk.

"Good afternoon, Miss Cook or is it Mrs.? I'm Braden Becker, a reporter for the *New York Star-Press.* I'm here to talk to you about Senator Margaret Hudson. You'll forgive the direct approach, but I understand she has hired you and I want to know just what she is hiding from the citizens of New York State."

"Uh, it's Miss," was the first thing Charlie could think of to say, even as a dozen thoughts ran through her brain. The reporter had certainly caught her off guard as he burst into the office, but the biggest reason for her confusion was that the man standing in front of her was the same one who had rescued her from the fire last night.

◉◉◉

Now in the full light of day, Charlie got her first good look at the reporter. Between the smoke, dark and her admittedly rattled brain, last night had been a bit of a blur. The voice, however, had been distinctive and she had no doubt this was the same man from the night before. With his glasses and slightly bookish appearance she could see that he bore a strong resemblance to the comedian Harold Lloyd. Not exactly a heartthrob, but then this was business.

"Mr. Becker, was it? Do you want to explain why you pushed your way into my office unannounced?" she asked while grabbing the letters off her desk and trying to put them into her desk as unobtrusively as possible.

"As I said I'm a reporter and I'm here to talk about the senator. I followed Miss Cleary here from the Kingery, so there's no use in denying it. I was right down the hall when she walked out of here."

Charlie silently cursed the meddlesome assistant who had been careless enough to lead the reporter right to her door.

"Really? How dramatic! But anyone who may or may not be a client is confidential. So if there's nothing else, you might as well leave," she said, standing up from behind her desk.

Becker smiled broadly. "Are you going to forcibly remove me? Because as fun as that might be, I would probably have to write a story about it. It's just the kind of scandalous headline our readers love: 'Senator's private eye attacks reporter.' It does have a certain ring to it."

Charlie groaned. "Listen, you can ask all the questions you want, but I have nothing to tell you."

The reporter plopped down in the client chair opposite the desk and pulled out his notebook. "Great, now let's start with why Miss Cleary was here."

She knew nosy reporters were a necessary evil in the private eye business, but this one was particularly annoying. "Wait, I didn't mean you could actually…"

"No changing the rules now, Miss Cook. By the way, you are certainly not what I expected. I saw the name Charlie Cook and figured the senator had hired a rumpled, alcoholic, middle-aged man. You, on the other hand, are certainly not that. You are certainly the most attractive private eye I've ever seen."

Oh, for the love of…was he actually trying to *flirt* with her? The sooner she got this idiot out of her office the better.

"Flattery will get you nowhere, Mr. Becker. I've heard it all before. 'A girl detective, how amazing!' Let me make it clear: I'm not answering any questions, so please…leave…now."

Becker shrugged his shoulders. "And I thought we were going to be friends. Well, I don't want to overstay my welcome, then. But I will be in touch. Whatever is going on with the senator, my readers have the right to know."

I just know this guy is going to be a problem, she thought as she watched the reporter leave. Fully expecting him to be lurking somewhere outside the office, she waited ten minutes before leaving to visit Nan's, the coffee shop where she expected to find Peter Leister, the head of the union.

◉◉◉

Braden Becker was, in fact, doing his best to hide just across the street from the rather dilapidated building where Charlie Cook had her office on the second floor. Luckily, he thought, there was only the one front door, so she couldn't leave without him being able to spot her. After all, it's not like she was going to climb out the window and leap from rooftop to rooftop, he thought with a smile.

That smile grew as he thought about the detective. There was something about her he liked. Sure, she was beautiful, but the tough attitude was an even bigger attraction. *Dammit, focus. You've got a job to do*, he thought.

The truth was he felt slightly unsavory chasing the senator's dirty laundry. For all his bluff and bluster, he really didn't care about the senator's personal life and didn't think it was anyone else's business either. Unfortunately, his publisher didn't share his opinion. A recent hire from William Randolph Hearst's *New York American*, he was a full-on believer in the church of yellow journalism and believed it was the best way to save the failing *Star-Press*. He had sent Becker to Washington with the instructions not to come back unless he came up with an exclusive story on the senator.

"She was a damn chorus girl," he had said. "There's no way in hell she doesn't have something in her background that will embarrass the Democrats."

So that, thought Becker, *is how someone goes from dreams of a Pulitzer to peering in windows like a creeping, peeping Tom.*

"Enough feeling sorry for yourself," he said as he saw Charlie Cook emerge from the building. "Let's see where the detective is going."

⊙⊙⊙

Charlie glanced up and down the street as she emerged from the front door. As she expected, there was that reporter, actually trying to hide in the doorway of the old shoe store across the street.

This could be fun…but let's see how long he can manage to stay with me. He should really get to see the sights here in the neighborhood.

Charlie proceeded to lead Becker on a guided tour of first the Lincoln Dress Shop, then the Chase Hardware Store. Each time she saw him trying to find new hiding spots up and down the street. It was while she was at the hardware store that she saw what she had been waiting for: The No. 12 streetcar. She dashed out of the store, her quick exit not prompting even a glance from Mr. Chase, who had seen the detective do lots of strange things over the years.

She hopped on the trolley just before it started moving again, then quickly pushed her way to the back of the car. She slipped out the rear door as it pulled away. She glanced back to make sure Becker was on the trolley. As it crested the hill and began to build up speed she could see him looking around frantically for her before spotting her on the street. She gave him a smile and a wave before ducking around the corner. One street over she caught the bus that would get her to Nan's.

⊙⊙⊙

"No changing the rules now, Miss Cook".

After all that effort, though, the visit to the union leader had been worthless, with the exception of giving her a good workout. Two gorillas stood up to greet her as soon as she said she wanted to speak to Leister.

"Well now, what do you want to speak to the boss about, little lady?" Gorilla No. 1 said, looking her up and down with a salacious grin on his face. "Maybe I can help you out."

"No thanks. I need to talk to Leister about that fire at the Coal Association's office."

That wiped the grin off of the greeter's face. "Scram, lady. The boss isn't taking any visitors. He already spent the whole day talking to them cops, so you can just make like a tree and leave."

Gorilla No. 2 snorted. "Like a tree, that's a good one, George."

"Shut up, Marv," he said before turning back to Charlie. "Now, like I says before, you need to go away." He cracked his knuckles for emphasis.

"Ooh, that's a nice touch, George," Charlie said. "Cracking the knuckles, very menacing. Now, why don't you let Mr. Leister know I'm here and he can decide if he wants to talk to me. I assume he's in that office back there?"

"Come on, lady," George said. "This doesn't have to get ugly. We don't want to hurt no dame. Just turn around and make it easy for everyone."

Charlie smiled. "You know, I was going to say the same thing, except that you should get out of the way and make it easy for everyone. I'm an animal lover and I'd hate to have to hurt two lower primates."

"I think that's an insult, George…"

"Shut up, Marv. Of course it is, she's saying we're a couple of apes." He turned back to Charlie. "Last chance. Get out. Now." He took one menacing step toward Charlie, then put his hand on her shoulder in an attempt to turn her around.

Charlie figured that the two behemoths counted on their size to intimidate most people without a fight. She also knew from past experience that she could use their strength against them. She slipped her shoulder away from George's grip and spun away from him.

He stepped toward her again, swinging a punch at her, but Charlie easily dodged it, pivoting on her heel and delivering a sharp kick to his stomach. He doubled over in pain, but Marv was already coming at her from the side. She spun around, her leg connecting with his jaw. He staggered backwards, dazed by the impact.

George was still on his feet, though, and he came at her with renewed fury, swinging wildly. She ducked and dodged, her movements graceful and precise as she avoided his blows. Finally, she saw an opening and lunged forward, delivering a series of quick punches and kicks that sent him crashing to the ground.

But Marv was still on his feet, and he came at her with a roar of anger. She braced herself, ready to take him on. He was big and powerful, but she was faster and more agile, dodging his blows and landing powerful kicks that sent him staggering backward. Reaching behind her she grabbed a metal coffee pot off the counter. She smashed it against Marv's head, where it connected with a satisfying thud. He went down like a sack of potatoes, unconscious.

To her right she saw George, now armed with a .45. With no time to spare, she spun around, her leg extended in a roundhouse kick that connected with his wrist. The gun went flying across the room as he cried out in pain, clutching his injured limb.

"Enough!"

Charlie turned to see a fiftyish man, gray haired, with the beginning of a belly, standing in the now-open doorway of the office. Leister looked at his two bodyguards on the floor of the shop, shaking his head in disgust.

"Was this really necessary? You've made quite a mess here."

Charlie shrugged her shoulders and straightened the sleeves on her slightly disheveled shirt. "I just wanted to talk to you, Mr. Leister. Just a few questions about that fire at the Winwood. It was your two…associates that decided to make things difficult."

Leister sighed, put his hands on his hips and shook his head again.

"That's what this was about? I'll tell you the same thing I told the cops. We had nothing to do with it. I don't know anything about the fire. There's no upside for us. We're trying to get Congress to vote for our bill. Blowing up offices isn't the way to win that type of fight.

"Now, if you'll excuse me, I've got to go hire some new bodyguards."

◉◉◉

On the way back to her office, she stopped at the Western Union office to see if there was any news from Harry Berg, her New York detective friend. There was, but none of it was good. He had finally found the shutterbug that took the compromising photos of the senator. Unfortunately, he was a resident of Cypress Hills Cemetery and had been for more than a decade.

The photographer had only one living relative, a nephew that apparently lived somewhere out west. There was no information about what had happened to any of his photographs after his death. Berg asked if he should continue looking for information or give up on the investigation.

Charlie wired him back to thank him for his work but to tell him to stop searching. Most likely the pictures had just ended up in someone else's hands years ago and the photographer had nothing to do with it.

Well, that's another dead end—literally. With dark approaching, Charlie decided it was time to find out more about what Braden Becker knew—but that was a goal better accomplished by the Black Wraith.

◎◎◎

It hadn't taken Charlie long to figure out that the New York reporter was staying at the Bainbridge Hotel. It was just about the closest hotel to the Kingery that someone working on a newspaperman's budget could afford. A visit to the front desk and some batted eyes at the desk clerk had revealed that Becker was in room 312.

A quick reconnaissance had confirmed that the lone window for the room was visible from the alley, so that's where the Black Wraith found herself that night, waiting in the darkness. Moving shadows confirmed that the room was occupied, but she preferred to wait until her target had gone to sleep. Catching a drowsy subject off guard always produced better results.

The Black Wraith waited another twenty minutes after the lights went out before easing her way to the back door and rear stairway she had found earlier. It was a relatively simple endeavor to make it to the reporter's hotel room without being spotted and she easily defeated the simple lock on the door.

Becker sat up as soon as she turned the switch to light up the room, springing to attention, then letting out a yell when he saw the black shape leaning against the doorframe. He scrambled for his glasses, grabbing them from the bedside table.

The reporter's eyes widened as he recognized the figure standing in his doorway. "What the...you! But how did you...I mean, what do you..."

The Black Wraith chuckled, pushing herself away from the doorframe and sauntering into the room. "Ahh, a girl does so like to be remembered, Mr. Becker. I think it's time we had a little chat. I believe you have some information that might be of interest to me."

The reporter looked down at the sheet covering the bottom half of his body, then colored slightly. "Uh, sure...but, uh...do you mind giving me a minute to get dressed. I'm actually, well..."

"Come now, turnabout seems like fair play. As I remember, you enjoyed the eyeful you got last night at Winwood."

The pink of Becker's cheeks darkened to a deep scarlet.

"Oh my, so shy? Here, put these on," the Black Wraith said with another chuckle, tossing him a pair of pants that had been strewn across the chair, that with its companion desk were the only other pieces of furniture in the sparsely decorated room. She waited for him to pull the pants on before continuing.

"Now, let's talk about last night—what were you doing at the Winwood?"

"Uh uh, I'm not answering your questions until I get answers to my questions."

"Yeah, that's not how this works, Mr. Becker. I ask the questions, you answer them."

"And why should I answer your questions? I mean, you're just some woman who shows up in my hotel room wearing a rather tight black outfit."

"Thanks for noticing, but that's not the point. The reality, Mr. Becker, is that if I wanted to I could hurt you. Trust me, do a little checking yourself and you'll probably be able to find some stories about me. But the truth is, that's not the way I like to operate."

She paused, tilting her head in thought.

"Maybe we can help each other, then. You want a story. I want information. It would seem that there could be a mutually beneficial relationship here."

"Well, that sounds promising," Becker replied, winking at her.

"A business relationship, Becker. Don't get any other ideas."

Becker faked a frown, then sighed deeply. "Fine then. What did you have in mind?"

"I need to take care of a problem that you're involved in. If I can solve this problem, and you stay out of my way, I can promise you a story. Deal?"

Becker nodded in agreement. "Done."

"So here's what I know, Becker. You're chasing a story on the senator—and somehow that led you to the Coal Association's office last night. I thought maybe you had started the fire, but having found out a little more about you today, I'm willing to give you the benefit of the doubt. So what *were* you doing there?"

"Honestly," Becker responded. "I thought maybe you had started the fire. But I did my own checking today. I heard stories about this mysterious black-clad woman who seems to show up at various places across the city when there's trouble. No one seems to know much about her and the reporter I talked to said there's never been a story written about you because there's no proof you exist. It's nice to know you're real, at least."

"You didn't answer my question."

"Oh, sorry. Well, my editor sent me here to investigate the senator. He's got it in his head that there's something going on. I'd been in town for six days and hadn't found much of anything. In fact, I was ready to head back to New York, but then I got a note slipped under my door that sent me there."

"Do you still have the note?"

"Yeah, it's…uh, over there, in my satchel," he said pointing at the bag sitting on the desk. "Is it all right if I…"

The Black Wraith nodded and waved her hand in the direction of the desk. Becker moved over there and quickly rummaged through the bag before pulling out a sheet of paper and passing it over. The handwritten note had been scrawled on a piece of stationary bearing the name of the Bainbridge Hotel.

Mr. Becker
The information you want about the senator can be found at the offices of the American Coal Association. Go tonight, as the files will be removed tomorrow. Hurry if you want to get the answers.

There was something about the note that seemed vaguely familiar to the Black Wraith. It was probably the similarity in language to the notes sent to the senator. But why handwrite this one? Somebody had been in a hurry to get Becker the message.

"I assume this stationary is easy to come by?"

"Yes, there's a pad in the desk and probably every other room in the hotel. Anyway, I went that night and arrived just in time to see you trying to pick the lock on the door. I was watching you when the door blew out and, well, you know the rest. Now why were you there?"

"I'm investigating the senator myself, along with the mines; let's just leave it at that. Have you learned anything else?"

Becker shared background about the pending mine safety bill in the Senate. The Black Wraith feigned interest, although there was no new information there for her. It seemed Becker had uncovered little besides that there was someone who wanted people to believe the senator was crooked. It was a possibility that she had to consider herself, as it would explain a lot of what was happening.

"I haven't found any evidence that she's been doing anything illegal and I have to say I don't see any upside for her," Becker said. "She's wealthy; she's not running for the seat in the fall. What would she have to gain? But then I've seen plenty of people break the law for the slightest gain.

"There is one more thing you should know, though. I'm pretty sure the senator has hired a private detective, but I'm not sure why. Her name's Charlie Cook. She—"

The Black Wraith let a touch of ice into her voice. "Oh, yes, I know Miss Cook. She's a meddler, that's for certain, but she won't be a problem. I've already taken care of her."

Becker's eyes widened at that. "Whoa, wait a minute, you didn't—"

"No, no, no. I didn't kill her if that's what you're thinking. Settle down. I just had a short, direct chat with her. I made it clear she needed to stay out of my way." She let the cold fury creep back in. "Speaking of which, remember our deal, Becker. I prefer to avoid violence as long as everyone is agreeable."

Becker laughed nervously. "Hey, I'm no hero. Just trying to keep my job."

"I'm glad to hear it. I'll be watching you, Mr. Becker. Don't disappoint me." And with that, she turned and slipped out of the room as silently as she had entered.

Becker let out a sigh of relief as the door clicked shut behind her. He had no idea what he was going to do, but one thing was certain—he may not be giving up on his story, no matter what he had told the Black Wraith, but he was going to have to be a lot more careful.

◉◉◉

Exhausted and battered from two days of being attacked, nearly roasted and blown up, and probably concussed at least one, now the Black Wraith found her way back to the alley. Just the thought of making her way home on foot left her exhausted. *Tonight, I'm going to use some of the senator's money to take a cab home.*

Within seconds she had stripped off her mask and outfit, returning them to the small pouch she used for such instances, again appearing to be nothing more than a young woman out late at night. Despite the late hour, she managed to find a driver within a few minutes.

The cabbie attempted to engage her in conversation, but Charlie wasn't in the mood for talking. Even noting his youthful handsomeness and charming smile, she just didn't have the energy to engage in any flirtatious banter tonight. He finally gave up the effort, although he continued to steal glances at the back seat as they made the short ride to her building.

Starting to get worried about her safety, even on the nearly deserted streets, she spoke up. "Under other circumstances, I'd appreciate the attention, but keep the eyes on the road, OK?"

"Yeah, sorry," he said, turning a bright red that caused Charlie to smile. He must be even younger than she had thought. Now, she felt a little bad. He was friendly enough. "Hey, no hard feelings. I'm just exhausted tonight."

The driver just nodded and they made the rest of the drive in silence.

After the usual "Are you sure you want to be dropped off here?" conversation with the cab driver, Charlie made her way inside the building and to the apartment. When she thought about it later, Charlie would blame her fatigue for her nearly fatal mistake. Normally ultra-attentive to her surroundings, she was that night lost in her thoughts, replaying the last two days as she stepped into the apartment.

It was by only a fraction of a second that she dropped to the floor as the shot rang out. As she heard the bullet hit her solid wooden door, she flashed back to a memory of the lock feeling "off" as she had entered the apartment.

With the flash of the gun having briefly illuminated the shooter, Charlie flew across the small room. Her assailant had obviously expected his single shot to get the job done as he stood unmoving across the apartment. He crashed to the floor under her assault, but quickly recovered, pushing her off of him. Light leaked in from the streetlight outside her window and Charlie estimated he had at least six inches and a hundred pounds on her. With minimal space to move in the apartment and her exhausted state, she knew she needed to make quick work of him.

Now back on his feet, the intruder lunged at her, his massive fist aimed straight for her face. But she was quick, dodging the blow and delivering a swift punch to his gut.

The man let out a grunt of pain, but didn't back down. He swung at her again, and this time she was not able to dodge in time. The blow connected with her jaw, sending her flying across the room.

Charlie landed hard on the floor, her head spinning. She quickly got to her feet, but he was already across the room, attempting to wrap her in his bear-like embrace. With a swift elbow strike to the man's gut, she broke free from his grasp. She quickly turned to face him, her stance low and ready for battle.

As a knife appeared in his hand, Charlie, not for the first time, questioned her aversion to guns and other weapons that might have made this go more quickly. He lunged at her with the knife, but she was too quick for

...as a knife appeared in his hand.

him, dodging his attack and delivering a powerful roundhouse kick to his face.

The man stumbled backwards, his nose bleeding and his knife clattering to the ground. But he was not done yet. He straightened to a full standing position, then pulled out another knife and began to slowly circle as he planned his attack.

"Oh, you have got to be kidding me!" Charlie said, wondering just how many weapons this guy had with him. "I don't suppose you'd like to give up?"

The man let out a laugh, his eyes filled with malice. "You think a little girl like you can stop me?" he sneered. He looked her up and down appreciatively, seeming to notice her looks for the first time, as a creepy smile crossed his face. "Although I guess you're not that little, huh? When we're done, maybe I'll have a little fun with you."

Charlie shuddered, then held up her hand. "Wait, let me get this straight. As far as I can tell, you were sent here to kill me, so 'done' would seem to indicate that I'm dead. So just so I understand—and let's be clear here—your plan is to kill me and *then* have some fun with me? That's a little sick, don't you think? On the other hand, if you're going to be touching me, I think being dead would be preferable. I mean have you looked in a mirror? You must have a heck of a time getting a date…"

"Shut up!" he yelled as he charged at her, reacting in blind anger as she had hoped. Her first kick knocked the knife out of his hand, then she delivered a series of quick punches and kicks to his chest and stomach. He fell to the ground, groaning in pain.

"She said it would be easy," he said as he tried to sit up, just before her foot connected with his chin, sending him flat onto his back, his head hitting the floor with a loud thud.

"Wait, 'she'? Who?" Charlie asked as she crouched over the man, but he was out cold. Two slaps to his face didn't wake him up. "Well, that's damn inconvenient."

She got to her feet and turned the light on, groaning when she saw the damage. "That was my favorite chair, you dumb ox," she said, giving the shooter a kick to emphasize the point. A quick search of his jacket pockets revealed no additional weapons, but no identifying documents, either. She sighed as she prepared to check his pants pockets, remembering his earlier comments.

She verified that he was still unconscious. "This is the most you're getting from me, buddy," she muttered as she turned out the pockets. Nothing there, either, except for a small scrap of paper with her name and address written on it in blocky text.

She stood, stretching to work out the kinks in her back, then walked over to the phone, one of the few luxuries she splurged on. She asked the operator to connect her to the familiar number.

"Uncle Kenny?" she said when she heard the answer on the other end. "I had a visitor tonight and need some help getting things cleaned up."

⊚⊚⊚

Two uniformed Metropolitan Police Department officers were the first on the scene, and they handcuffed and dragged out the still-groggy attacker. Detective Walker had arrived only minutes later and taken her to the station where the shooter was being held.

"Well, your attacker was Freddie Keys," he had said as they drove. "I recognized him right away. Your typical, low-level freelance troublemaker and leg-breaker. He'll work for anyone who will pay him. He got out of jail about six months ago after four years in. He had disappeared since he got out, but we figured he was still causing trouble, just being more careful. Looks like we were right."

Now, she was waiting in the bullpen while Walker questioned Keys. Her request to join the questioning had been roundly rejected. "I'd like to keep my badge, Charlie," Walker had said when she asked.

In a dull gray, dimly lit room just down the hall, Walker sat across a small table from Keys, who was still handcuffed. The room was sparsely furnished with only the metal table and two chairs, and the overhead fluorescent light flickered occasionally. Keys sat calmly, his hands folded in front of him on the table. His suit was disheveled, his hair was mussed, and his face bore the telltale results of the tussle, but his eyes were cold and emotionless, and he exuded a sense of boredom.

"I got nothing to say, detective."

"Let's not pretend, Keys. You're an enforcer, a problem-solver. We both know that. But murder for hire is a new one. And boy, did you pick a bad target for this one. Not only was Charlie clearly more than you can handle, you should also know that her father was my best friend in the world, so let's try this again. Who hired you?"

Keys's eyes widened slightly at that information, but he quickly wiped his face clean of emotion once again.

"I already told ya, I got nothing to say."

Detective Walker stood up, his chair scraping against the concrete floor as he pushed it back. He leaned over Keys, his face inches from the suspect's. "Wrong answer. I think we're going to let you sit in here for a while and think about your future."

"It don't matter how long I sit here. You ain't getting anything else from me, copper."

Walker turned and smiled as he opened the door, raising his voice, ensuring it carried down the hall. "But it's for your own protection, Freddie. Now that you've told us everything we need to know about who hired you, it won't be safe for you to be in jail with the rest of the criminals. You know how they feel about informants."

Keys tried to stand, but the chained cuffs allowing him to only rise slightly. "You can't do that, detective! I ain't no rat! Get back here!" he yelled as Walker slammed the door shut on his cries.

Detective Walker reported back to Charlie about the lack of progress with Keys, but that he hoped the threat of branding him as a stoolpigeon would prompt more cooperation.

"I'm going to give him an hour or two to think about it, then we'll see if he's in a mood to be more forthcoming," he told her as they at his desk.

Charlie stood up. "That's OK. I think I've got this one pretty much figured out, Uncle Kenny. I just need to go to talk to the senator again. It's nearly 8 a.m. and I think my client has some questions to answer."

Walker shook his head. "Wait, Charlie. Haven't you been through enough in the last few days? Can't you wait until we get some more answers here?"

Charlie held her hands out and smiled innocently. "Just talking, Uncle Kenny. I don't even have any extra clothes with me, if you get my drift."

Walker groaned. "That's something, I guess. Just be careful."

Charlie continued walking out, before calling back over her shoulder. "When am I not careful?"

The detective sat down at his desk with a sigh. "'When am I not careful?' Forest, you owe me big time, my friend," he said, looking heavenward. "You raised a great girl, but damn it she is a pain in my ass sometimes."

◎◎◎

The desk clerk gave Charlie a disdainful look. Whether because she was Asian, a woman or simply not dressed like she belonged at the Kingery was hard to say.

"As I already told you...miss," he said with a sneer. "The senator is not to be disturbed. Miss Cleary left clear instructions this morning."

He turned away from the detective, pretending to busy himself by shuffling papers on the rear counter. Charlie stared at his back for a few seconds, pushing down the urge to jump across the desk and throttle the man. She then pivoted herself and walked quietly out of the hotel, determined not to draw any more attention. There was, after all, more than one way to make her way to the senator's suite.

She exited and, when she was sure the doorman wasn't looking, slipped down the small alley that ran alongside the building. She turned the corner the rear of the Kingery and, as she hoped she would, found one of the kitchen staff smoking outside the service entrance.

The woman, one of the waitresses Charlie surmised from her clothing, glanced up at her. She looked way too young to have such tired eyes, Charlie thought.

"You looking for something?" she asked the detective.

Charlie smiled. "Would you believe I just want to get in the building?"

The waitress looked back at her. "Sure. You think you're the first woman I've seen sneak in through the backdoor? Although usually it's at night... somebody must be feeling frisky this morning!"

Charlie was about to protest, then decided to roll with it. "Well, hey, you gotta do what you gotta do."

The waitress shook her head. "Tell me about it," she said with a tired smile. "But go ahead and go on in. No skin off my nose."

Charlie stepped past her, then paused when the woman spoke again. "Hey, if you're going up, you better take the rear stairs so the house dick or that prissy jerk at the desk doesn't spot you. Follow the hall when you go in, then take the first right. Stairs will be right there."

Charlie thanked her and headed inside. Following her instructions, she was able to easily find her way to the 12th floor. It took the senator only a moment to answer after Charlie knocked.

"Oh, Miss Cook," the senator said when she opened the door, her shock showing on her face. "I thought we agreed to keep our distance while you worked on the case. I, well...fine, come inside then. Don't need you standing here in the hall."

The senator led her into the same room they had sat in before, but this time there was no offer of a drink.

"Does this mean you've figured out who is behind those letters I've been getting?"

Charlie nodded, "Oh yes, I understand everything now. Is Miss Cleary here?" she asked.

"Yes, but I'm afraid she's taken ill. The poor thing is asleep in her room," the senator said, gesturing in that direction.

"Mmm, well that's just as well, I suppose. It will give you time to get your story straight."

The senator turned back toward Charlie, the anger clear on her face. "My story? Just what is that supposed to mean?"

Charlie responded loudly. "Considering I've almost been killed at least twice, I think I'm the one who gets to be upset here."

Now, the older woman looked more confused than angry. "What are you talking about?"

"Well, let's see," Charlie said, ticking points off on her fingers. "Ever since I took the case, there's clearly been a number on my head. You tell me to go to the Coal Association's office, there's a fire there. I visit the union reps, and they're clearly poised to give me a beating."

Charlie's voice continued to rise in volume. "Then, last night I get back to my apartment and there is someone waiting there to kill me. He was unsuccessful, as you can clearly see, but a person can only take so many attempts on their life. By the way, my visitor last night happened to mention that it was a woman who hired him. Apparently, she told him I would be an easy target."

The senator collapsed in the chair, looking shocked. "I swear…I don't know what you're talking about. I…I hired you to find out…were you really attacked?"

Charlie nodded, but her eyes were no longer on the senator. "I know, senator. Glad to see I was loud enough to get your attention," she said, looking at Cleary, who was now standing ten feet behind the senator, a look of disgust on her face.

"I knew I should have been worried when I didn't hear from that idiot," she said.

Charlie took one step toward her, but stopped when Cleary raised her hand, pointing a small revolver in her direction.

"Selena, what…why?" the senator said, struggling to get the words out.

"'Selena, what…Selena why'," Cleary said in a high-pitched voice. "Why don't you ask the girl detective here? I'm curious to know how much she figured out."

Charlie shrugged her shoulders. "Pretty much what I said to the senator, except that I figured it had to be you. There were two women who knew I'd been hired and could set me up to get knocked off. There was no reason for the senator to hire me and then try to kill me. You made it clear all along that you were against hiring me. Oh, and you made one more mistake. That hand-written note you left for Braden Becker. I recognized your writing from the note you gave me that day you came to my office. Sloppy, sloppy.

"Now why you care about mining regulations, I have no idea and really don't care."

Cleary laughed at that. "It was never about the coal mines. That was just a nice distraction to get people all riled up. You know, one of the great things about legislation is that you can always find a nice, long, complicated bill and stick a little something in there that no one notices. Everybody is always packing these full of little presents for the constituents back home and no one ever reads the whole package. Democracy is a beautiful thing."

"So this wasn't about the mines at all?" the senator asked.

Cleary rolled her eyes. "Yes, try to keep up." She looked at Charlie. "Maybe there's something to that whole 'women shouldn't hold public office' idea, huh? When we eliminated your husband, we were hoping you'd be easier to manipulate, but here we are.

"Anyway, if you must know, it gives a little group I'm associated with some extra potential influence. Just a little budget allocation to carve out a little role for one of our members in the war department—something we think might be necessary down the road."

She turned back toward the senator, now pointing the gun toward her. "Luckily, we no longer need your vote, senator. You were just one of several potential shall we say, 'allies' we were working on and I've been told we have what we need now."

Charlie had managed to inch closer during the woman's diatribe, but she still would probably not be able to disarm Cleary without the senator getting hurt. The best plan, she figured, was to keep the woman talking.

"So what's your end game here?"

Cleary swung the weapon back in her direction. "You've been a big help there. The desk clerk and who knew who else saw you down in the lobby—he called up here after they kicked you out, as per my instructions. It's a tragic tale, you see. You, a seedy detective, were attempting to blackmail the senator—why, we've got the letters right here—and when she wouldn't pay up, you shot her. Luckily, her loyal assistant was here and managed to kill you. But alas, it was not in time to save the senator. Just another wily, sinister Oriental trying to take advantage of a good white woman."

She turned toward the senator and as her finger tightened on the trigger, Charlie leapt at the senator, knocking her down. At the same time, she seemed to fade, becoming almost translucent. Without the dark, she wasn't completely invisible, but it was enough to momentarily freeze Cleary on place.

"What the…" was all she got out before Charlie—fully visible again—slammed into the taller woman. Her first hit sent the gun skittering across the room, where it slid under one of the chairs, disappearing from view. They collapsed to the floor, a tangle of limbs.

Cleary recovered quickly, though, delivering a chop to Charlie's ribs, then pushing her away and rolling free. Both women sprang to their feet. Charlie was the first to regain her footing, quickly delivering a series of quick punches and kicks, but Cleary managed to dodge and block most of them.

"You think you're the only one who knows how to fight?" she sneered at Charlie.

Cleary, using her advantage in size and strength, managed to grab Charlie's arm and twist it behind her back. But Charlie managed to spin out of the hold and deliver a powerful roundhouse kick to Cleary's face. Cleary stumbled back, dazed, but managed to stay on her feet.

Charlie, seeing her opportunity, rushed forward, but Cleary was ready this time. She sidestepped and delivered a powerful punch to Charlie's face, sending her crashing to the ground. As Charlie rolled to her feet again, Cleary ran for the door. She reached it, but wasn't able to open it before Charlie crashed into her again, the impact carrying both women out into the hall.

"What the hell is going on?" they both heard, looking up to see two beefy men standing in the hall, clearly hotel security.

"Thank god you're here," Cleary said, gasping. "This woman attacked us. You have to protect me! I think she killed the senator!"

"What?" asked the same man who had spoken before, as he ran into the suite. The other grabbed Charlie, holding tight.

"I'm going to get a doctor," Cleary said, taking off down the hall.

"Let me go!" Charlie said, trying to free herself from the man's grip. "She's the one who attacked the senator!"

"All right, settle down, lady. She works for the senator. I don't know who you are."

"Fine, just remember you made me do this," she said, punching the man in the stomach then delivering another blow to his face, leaving him dazed. Charlie sprinted for the stairs. She ran all the way to the first floor, but

Cleary was gone by the time she reached the ground, nowhere to be seen.

"That's her!" she heard shouted behind her, turning to see three guards running in her direction. She threw up her arms in surrender as they closed in.

◎◎◎

Two nights later, Charlie was sitting—happily free—in the living room of the Walker apartment. She had endured the well-meaning concern of Marie Walker during dinner, but it was now just Charlie and Detective Ken Walker relaxing in the living room of the couple's homey but happy apartment.

"You're just lucky the senator regained consciousness," Walker said. "Without her help, I'm not sure I would have gotten you out of that jail cell. Her backing up your story was a big help."

Charlie had managed to save the senator from being shot, but had also knocked her out in the process. But after one night in jail for her and one night in the hospital for the senator, everyone was back where they belonged. The senator had even made it back to the senate where, she had vowed to Charlie, she would make sure the bill didn't pass, the consequences be damned.

"I'd feel a lot better if Cleary hadn't gotten away," Charlie said. "But she's a ghost—no one saw her after she ran down the hall. She just disappeared. I just wish I knew what had happened to her."

◎◎◎

The woman who had spent the last several months known as Selena Cleary warily stepped into the darkened room. The woman waiting there looked at her with an unreadable expression on her face. Tall, regal of bearing, and breathtakingly beautiful, she was known by those who worked for her simply as the Countess.

Cleary knew that the punishment for failing the Countess and her mysterious organization was often death, but she was prepared to accept whatever her leader said she deserved. That was the agreement she had made when the Countess had plucked her from the streets of Baltimore years ago and made her into what she was today. She looked down at the ground as she approached.

"I sense your fear, my child," the Countess said, reaching for Cleary's face and lifting it to look her in the eyes. "You, who are my most trusted operative—someone I trained from nothing into the perfect specimen you are today. What have you to fear from me?"

"I failed you," she replied.

"In a way. True, I am disappointed, but the future is constantly in motion. Even in our defeats we have achieved an important victory."

"A victory?"

"Why yes," the Countess said. "A truly important one, I believe. This one they call the Black Wraith has thwarted us on more than one occasion. At first, she didn't worry me, but now, she has become more than a mere annoyance.

"But thanks to you, we now know she is Charlie Cook. The Black Wraith was an enigma, a ghost that we couldn't reach. She disappeared into the safety of darkness. Charlie Cook is no mystery. She is someone who has friends, a life. Someone who is vulnerable.

"You have a new mission, my child. The time has come. Destroy the Black Wraith."

THE END

BEHIND THE MASK

Charlie Cook AKA The Black Wraith is well on her way to becoming my favorite character. This is her first standalone adventure since she made her debut in a Red Jackal tale a few years ago and she is, quite simply, just fun to write.

Sometimes stories just come from two facts that rattle around in my head until they find each other. That's what happened here.

Fact 1: There's a long history of widows being appointed to finish out terms of their deceased husbands dating back to the early 1900s. Usually, these appointments have been for short periods of time until a new election could be held.

Fact 2: In 2022, there was a congressional candidate that caused some controversy because of her brief past as a stripper during college. And there we are. These "widow's successions" have rarely been controversial and the appointed replacement has not often had to weigh in on important matters, but what if one had to make a key vote…and she had a bit of a history that could be leveraged? Enter Charlie Cook.

◉◉◉

JONATHAN W. SWEET - is an award-winning journalist and the author of eight books. He is the founder of Brick Pickle Pulp, which publishes books in the classic pulp style and the host of the weekly Pulp Nostalgia & Old Time Radio Podcast. In 2020 he was named to the "Who's Who in New Pulp."

He is a two-time finalist for the Pulp Factory Awards. Both volumes of his *Beginner's Guide to Pulp Fiction* were Amazon No. 1 New Releases and reviewers have called his books "essential," "invaluable" and "captivating."

Jonathan lives in the Twin Cities with his wife, two exceptional children and one fairly dim-witted dog. Find more on Jonathan at JonathanWSweet.com and BrickPickleMedia.com.

THE DEVIL TAKES A BRIDE

By Mark Allen Vann

She felt her knees buckle as the panic fully set in. The hand which gripped her throat grew tighter and her vision began to dim. She knew she was as good as dead. The last thing she felt before the blackness set in was a sudden jarring; the last thing she saw was her would-be killer's head explode apart in a blossom of blood and gore. Then she collapsed next to his corpse—

She woke up in a daze, not knowing where she was. She looked up into the face of a handsome man with a pencil thin mustache. He wore a top dollar pinstripe suit complete with a black-banded fedora. He looked her over before thrusting a glass of bourbon at her. "Here, drink this. You have had quite a shock. There is little time and I need some answers."

The auburn-haired woman sat up unsteadily, confusion written on her face. "What? Who? Where am I?"

"I believe you are in your apartment. Now please get a grip on yourself. The gunshot and commotion had to have been heard by some of your neighbors, and the cops will be here soon. I need to put in some distance long before that."

The woman finally picked up the bourbon and took a gulp. Her eyes watered and her face scrunched into a grimace as the spirit burned its way down her throat. She looked at the man again and her eyes narrowed. "Who the hell are you and what happened to—" her voice trailed off as she saw the bloody remains of the corpse that was leaking all over her carpeting. "Oh—" She nearly fell back once again at the sight of the gruesome remains.

"So, tell me. How do you know Mullaney?"

Her brow furrowed. "Who?"

The man in the pinstripe suit nodded toward the body on the floor. "Roger Mullaney. He's the stiff that just redecorated your apartment with his gray matter. How do you know him?"

She downed the rest of the bourbon before continuing. "I never met him before today. He just came in here, and he—he got violent. You did not answer my question. Who are you?"

"He is a member of Saul Franchetti's goon squad. Or he was. Who *I* am does not matter at this moment. Now tell me, who are you and why does Saul Franchetti got a mad on for your hide?"

She gave the man a more appraising eye and realizing she was dealing with someone who was not fooling around, she decided to play it straight. "My name is Elaine Franchetti. I'm Saul Franchetti's wife."

Stephen Kildare stared down at the young lady and gasped. Things just took a very interesting turn.

◉◉◉

Stephen processed what the woman had said. "Do you want to run that by me one more time?"

"Saul Franchetti is my husband. Sort of." She gave him a sideways glance. "It's a bit complicated."

"Considering one of Saul's henchmen just tried to kill you, I would say it is. Look Miss—I mean Mrs. Franchetti, we need to get out of here. The police will be here any minute."

Elaine shook her head. "I don't understand. I don't even know who you are frankly, and I don't see why I need to leave."

Stephen sighed. "Let me put it bluntly. Saul, whether he is your husband or not, just sent a man to kill you. As soon as he finds out that his plan failed, he will try again."

Elaine got up and tilted her chin in petulant defiance. "So? The police will protect me when they see what has transpired."

Kildare began to lose his patience. "Look, lady. I used to work for Saul, and I know how he operates. And I know for a fact that a good portion of the police are in his back pocket. You wouldn't last a day in their protection."

She folded her arms over her chest and rolled her eyes. "And I suppose you are here to protect little Ol' me?"

"Yes, even if it means I have to take you over my knee first!" he growled.

Elaine's eyes grew wide, and she looked like she was about to give him a rebuttal when the sound of sirens in the distance silenced her.

Stephen ran to the window and peeked out. "Time's up, lady. Last chance. Grab what you need—we gotta go." He paused long enough to toss a cheap, plastic mask on the corpse and headed quickly to the apartment door.

Elaine hesitated briefly before her eyes gazed once again upon the corpse on the floor. She grabbed her purse and jacket and followed him. "Okay, okay you win!"

Stephen went out into the hallway and saw a couple of Elaine's neighbors poking their heads out of their doorways cautiously. They saw him come out, and they quickly shut their doors. The two made a beeline for the stairs. "My roadster is parked around the corner; we can head out the back. Let's go."

The sound of the sirens filled the air as two patrol cars screeched to a stop in front of the apartment building. But Stephen and Elaine were several blocks away in a fiery red roadster, which was Stephen's most prized possession.

Moments later they were speeding through the streets and leaving the apartment in the distance. "We need to find a place we can sit down and talk. I have more questions for you," Stephen said as he navigated through the city streets. "A lot more!"

◉◉◉

A couple hours later, Elaine sat on an uncomfortable folding chair in front of a shabby wooden table. She stared idly at an untouched glass of water which was unceremoniously placed in front of her.

"I'm sorry. I don't have much to offer you, I wasn't expecting company. I can fix you a sandwich if you're hungry," the man who had introduced himself to her as Kildare called out from what she assumed was the kitchen, in the tiny apartment he had taken her to.

"No thank you," she replied noncommittally. "Where are we, anyway?"

"Somewhere safe," he answered as he walked into the room with his hands full of cold cuts and dry bread. "This is one of the safehouses which I kept while I was working for your husband. Don't worry. He doesn't know about it. Nobody does."

She stared at him then. "I still don't get it, why would my husband send that man to—to—" Her voice died in her throat as she thought about just what the man had been sent there to do.

Stephen shook his head. "I don't know the answer to that. Heck, I never even knew he was married. My guess is you may have stumbled upon something that he didn't want you to know, and you became a liability."

"Stumbled upon something?" Elaine jumped to her feet. "What do you mean, Mr. Kildare?" She studied the stranger closer, her eyes falling upon the man's jacket which she knew concealed the gun which was used very recently. "Just what kind of work did you *do* for my husband?"

Stephen decided to try the direct approach with the woman. "I killed people. Lots of them."

Elaine slumped back into the chair—her eyes wide in shock.

Stephen realized then that she was clueless as to what kind of monster Saul Franchetti was. He sat down in the chair next to her and gave her a sympathetic look. "What do you know about your husband's business, Mrs. Franchetti?"

She gazed up at him slowly, shaking her head. "Not much, just that he is some sort of businessman. He never really talked about his work."

Kildare nodded. "He is a businessman all right. But his business is blood and death. He runs the largest organized crime family in the area. Until recently I was part of that family." Kildare paused and looked at the woman. "Though, despite working closely with him, I guess he still had a few surprises."

Elaine looked at him inquisitively. "If you didn't know he had a wife, then how did you know I needed to be saved?"

Kildare shook his head. "I didn't. I was tracking Mullaney to gather some information when the bastard came to visit you. I could tell he was up to no good, so I followed him here. Unfortunately, I had to shoot him before I could question him."

Elaine glanced at Kildare inquisitively. "Unfortunately?"

Stephen shrugged his shoulders absently as he placed a sandwich in front of his impromptu house guest. "Yeah. I didn't get a chance to ask him any questions." He made a similar sandwich for himself and devoured it in only a few bites before he continued. "Now tell me. How long have you and Saul been married?"

"I hardly think that is any of your concern," she replied haughtily as she finished off her sandwich. After a moment she peered up and held her rescuer's steely gaze. She nodded down at her newly emptied plate. "Thank you for the food. I guess I was hungry after all. Look, I don't mean to be rude, but I am having a hard time wrapping my head around what exactly is going on. One minute I am alone in my apartment and the next there is someone trying to kill me. Then you are there and shoot them—It's all just too much to imagine."

Kildare nodded compassionately. "I understand Mrs. Franchetti. I really do, but your life is in imminent danger and right now the only chance you have to get out of this in one piece is to help me, so I can help you. Do you understand?"

Elaine held Kildare's gaze once more, searching his eyes as if she were trying to delve into his very soul. After a pregnant pause, she nodded her head in mute recognition. "Very well, Mr. Kildare. I will level with you. Saul and I got married just over a year ago. It was very strange. Not a typical romantic affair. He didn't even want me to move into his house. He bought that apartment for me and sort of just let me be."

"So he courted you and married you and then ignored you?"

Elaine stared down aimlessly at her empty plate. "It wasn't like that. Not exactly. He didn't really do any courting. My father introduced us, and I guess he sort of arranged everything." She looked up at Kildare again and once again their eyes met. "He wasn't bad to me. He had one of his business associates check on me regularly and bring me anything I needed. I was well cared for. And he treated me nice on the occasions when he would come and call personally. But there was no romance and very little intimacy involved. And I guess—well I guess it was hardly the storybook ending I had always dreamed of—" Elaine's voice trailed off as she shook her head. "There I go being silly."

Stephen Kildare sat quietly for a few minutes as he absorbed everything she had told him. "Okay, so let me get this straight. Your father had arranged a marriage between you and Saul Franchetti. Then Saul left you high and dry to wile away your time in your own place. Yet you did not question your father or Saul on this peculiar arrangement?"

"Well, I did ask my father at first, and he told me that all would be explained in good time. And, well, Saul made it very clear from the onset that I was not to ask too many questions." Again she glanced at Kildare as she spoke and saw his brow knit. "Don't get me wrong. He never threatened me or anything. As I said, he treated me very well. But most of my time I was sitting here all alone, and I was getting so bored. And I must say I was getting curious—"

"So you began inquiring into your husband's business affairs?"

"I guess so. Not much, little questions here and there. I asked Sammy— he's the guy Saul sent over on occasion to look after me, but he just gave me a queer look and didn't say anything. So I asked the only other person I could think of."

"You asked your father?"

Elaine nodded. "I paid him a visit a couple nights ago. We had dinner at his house, and I was just dying to know what was going on. Well, I knew almost immediately that something was wrong. He never kept secrets before, and I could tell there was a lot he was not telling me. Finally, a phone call had come in, and he took it in his study. I knew I shouldn't have, but I had to know what was happening, so I listened in at the door. I didn't really understand much of what was said, but I had the distinct feeling that he was talking to Saul about some important matter. I heard him scribbling something down as he spoke. Eventually, the conversation ended, and he disconnected the call. I ran back into the dining room and waited for his return."

"You said that happened two nights ago?"

Elaine nodded again.

"And he never knew you were eavesdropping?"

She shook her head. "Not as far as I could tell. But he would not have done anything if he had. He is my father after all—"

Kildare gave her a level look. "Elaine, who exactly is your father, anyway?"

"He is Walter Fitzgerald."

Kildare arched an eyebrow. "The Congressman?"

Elaine nodded yet again. "Yes, that's him. Do you know him?"

"Only by reputation, I'm afraid." Kildare pondered the information that Elaine shared, and he did not like the way things were adding up. Congressman Fitzgerald had a reputation all right. It included kickbacks, bribery, extortion, and all sorts of nefarious activities, none of which were ever proven. And now it seems he was in bed with Saul Franchetti, or more accurately, his daughter was. He knew she had to have learned something she shouldn't have and that is why Saul sent Mullaney to silence her.

It was time to pay the Congressman a visit.

◉◉◉

To say Saul Franchetti was livid was to say that the '27 Yankees were a decent ball team. The veins on his forehead were purple lightning bolts as he boiled over in a barely contained rage. "Tell me again, Sully. I want to hear it one more time."

Sully Venkman blanched. He wanted to be anywhere else in the world but in front of his very angry boss—and he sure did not want to have to repeat to him what he just told him. Knowing that the longer he clammed up, the angrier Saul was going to get, he finally marshalled his little remaining courage and began again. "Well, as I said, boss. We found Mullaney sprawled out on the dame's carpet leaking from a large hole in his forehead."

Saul glared at his lieutenant. "And Elaine?"

Sully shook his head. "She was gone, boss. Vanished."

Saul picked up a heavy ashtray which sat at one corner of the desk. "Go on. Tell me again the rest of it, Sully."

Sully paused and took a deep breath. "There uh, was this cheap plastic mask lying on the corpse—"

"What kind of mask?" Saul inquired in a deadly whisper.

Sully visibly paled. "It—it was a–a devil mask, boss."

The crash of the ashtray slamming into the far wall echoed throughout the room, eliciting a shriek from Sully, which Saul ignored. "So Kildare has come home to roost, has he? I will gut him like a carp!" Saul glanced at his shaking underling with disgust. "Get a grip on yourself, Sully. And then go find Kildare and bring me his head!"

Sully nodded his head vigorously. Relieved to be out of his boss's clutches, he nearly ran for the door. He didn't quite reach it in time before Saul spoke again.

"Oh, one more thing. I expect my men to be made of sterner stuff. The next time I see you sniveling like a whipped dog, I will find me a new lieutenant. Now beat it, and while you are out there, fetch me my dear wife. We need to have a little chat!"

◉◉◉

Stephen Kildare was at a loss. He knew he needed to check out Elaine's story and investigate the Congressman's activities a bit closer. If he was involved in Saul's operation, then that made him part of this mess and therefore he became Kildare's problem. Still, he couldn't just murder a Congressman, particularly one who happened to be Elaine's father. At least, not anymore. No, this would take a bit more finesse, something which was not necessarily his forte. He decided he would pay the politician a visit and see what would happen. He figured if he and Saul were tight, then it would not be long before Saul sent his goon squad on the hunt. A shakeup of Saul's operation would prove to be telling.

He left his unexpected charge at the safehouse and made her promise to keep her head down until he returned. He only hoped she did what he said and did not bring any undue attention upon herself. That done, he drove his roadster across town to the Congressman's home. He parked in a back alley a couple of blocks from the large estate, knowing that his choice of wheels was not exactly inconspicuous. He had toyed with the idea of getting a vehicle that was more subtle, but he really did not want to part with the beauty.

He watched the front of Congressman Fitzgerald's home from the shadows of a nearby hedgerow for about fifteen minutes. There was nothing stirring from within as near as he could tell from the distance. Something felt off, and he did not want to jump into the middle of a situation unless he knew what he was getting into. He watched for a few minutes longer before he decided he was not going to get anywhere by standing in the shadows. His hand fell to the pistol he kept in his suit coat as he tread towards the front gate—a gate that was unlatched and moving slightly on its own in the shallow breeze. He gripped the butt of his pistol tighter as he inched forward.

He slipped through the gate, his eyes scanning in every direction for sign of an ambush. After a moment or two, he satisfied himself that there was nobody lurking in the dark waiting to plug a few holes in him, so he continued towards the front door. As he got closer, he noticed the door was also partially open. He heard a soft moan coming from inside. Again, concerned he was walking into a trap, he slipped to the side of the doorway and nudged the heavy wooden door open wider with his foot. After a moment, he peered carefully inside and saw the entryway. A man was lying on the floor just a few feet past the door, a sizable pool of blood was steadily growing beneath him. Other than his soft sobbing moans from the injured man, there was no sound coming from the interior of the estate.

Kildare slipped into the home and knelt before the man. A cursory inspection showed that the man was shot in the stomach and was rapidly bleeding out. The man's time was limited.

"What happened here?" he asked the man, mustering as much kindness as he was able.

"Hit squad, Franchetti's men," the man rasped. "They took him."

"The Congressman?" Kildare queried.

The man nodded weakly. "Yes, you need to find him. Save him—"

Kildare knew the poor sucker would not last much longer. "Do you know where they took him? Or why?"

The man shook his head. "They didn't say. Just find him and tell him—I'm sorry—"

The man let out a frothy bubble of red spittle and a last gasp of air escaped him before he lay still and stared off into the sightless distance.

"Damn," Kildare cursed to himself. "Now I have more questions than answers and nothing is adding up!" Kildare knew from the condition of the Congressman's lackey that the hit could not have been too long ago, and he gathered that he just missed the perpetrators. The estate was fairly secluded, but he figured that the noise of the gunfire was likely reported and that the police were probably on their way. He did not have much time.

"Ahh, Stephen. It looks like you have a little mess on your hands," the "corpse" spoke gleefully. Normally, being mocked by a dead man would tend to have a disconcerting effect on a person, but for Stephen Kildare, AKA Killdevil, it was not out of the ordinary.

"What do you want? I do not have time for this," Kildare replied to the corpse, which had a sick grin on its face.

"Tut, tut. Stephen. I merely want to tell you I'm rooting for you. After all, you promised me Saul's soul, and I am looking forward to collecting. His, and his entire organization's souls. Hell, the Congressman's too while you're at it. He's just as dirty."

"Maybe. That's still to be seen, now if you don't mind. I would like to get out of here before the cops show up—"

"Oh, Stephen, you sure can be a stick in the mud sometimes," the corpse continued. "Now that Elaine girl, I bet her soul is sickly sweet—"

"Shut the hell up! You will not talk about her—"

"Ohh, it sounds like you are getting sweet on Saul's wife. Are you looking to replace Lauren so soon?"

"Shut the hell up!" Stephen screamed again as he lashed out with his foot and kicked the dead man's head. He instantly regretted his rash action, though he fumed as the corpse continued to mock him with laughter.

Kildare took a few steps towards the door, expecting the police to arrive at any time. If the gunshot did not alert anyone, the disappearance of such an important figure would most certainly bring attention eventually. He paused at the entry way and gazed back in the house. Something Elaine had said earlier had stuck in his mind. He quickly moved about the over-sized house looking for one room in particular—the study.

He found the room he was looking for at the top of the stairs, third door on the left. The study was immaculately decorated, or at least it would have been had it not been ransacked and left in disarray. Papers, books and various mementos and ephemera were strewn about like so many children's discarded play toys. Kildare made his way around the rubble trying in vain to find what he was looking for. He found a small notebook lying near the desk, but unfortunately the top page was blank. He quickly thumbed through it, but the rest of the notebook was as empty as the front page. Kildare noticed some bit of torn paper still adhered to the glue of the spine, indicating that at least one page had been torn from the book.

He had remembered that Elaine made mention that she had overheard him scribbling something down while he was on the phone with Saul. But it seemed whatever was written there was lost to him. He still had no idea where they might have taken the Congressman, or what the connection between the politician and the mob boss might be.

Kildare heard sirens in the distance and knew his time was about up. He cast one more glance around the room and headed towards the door.

Kildare paused yet again and raced back to the notebook. He yanked out a sheet of paper from the back of the book and glanced around, finding a pencil stuck beneath the overturned desk chair. He put the torn piece of paper on top of the notebook began to furiously rub the pencil across the page as the sirens grew steadily closer in the distance.

The negative of the front page of the notebook began to show through onto his scribbled page. He was near ecstatic when the tracing turned into a series of letters, which quickly turned into a pair of words—one of which was awfully familiar. He had no clue what it meant, but he hoped that Elaine did. The sirens were just a block or so away, and he was out of time. He stuck the tracing in his jacket pocket and without a backward glance; he was out the door and running down the stairs.

He made it out the gate and back to his earlier hiding place among the hedgerows just as three squad cards pulled up to the front of Congressman Fitzgerald's estate.

Stephen sighed heavily. It was time to break the news to Elaine.

⊙⊙⊙

As expected, Elaine Fitzgerald did not take the news of her father's abduction well at all. The fact that the fingers pointed to her own husband as the abductor did not help in the matter. Stephen Kildare had to coax the young woman from marching off to the nearest police station, citing once more the amount of corruption which snaked its way through the long arm of the law. He pled his case with her that until they knew who they could trust, they would try things his way first. If that failed, then he agreed she would go to the cops.

It was not lost on him that Elaine's own disappearance and the dead body found in her home, were going to cast very interesting theories in the investigation. He hoped it would keep the detectives off balance long enough for him to find some answers on his own.

Speaking of answers, he knew it was time he had a talk with Elaine on what he discovered in the Congressman's study.

He went to the small sitting room in the front of the safehouse, where he found Elaine much as he left her. She was sitting on the couch with her legs folded up beneath her, her chin resting on one knee.

...whatever was written there was lost to him.

"Do you know someone by the name of Larchmont?" he asked as he sat down some soup and a glass of water before his young charge.

For a moment she did not respond. Kildare was about to ask again when she slowly roused from whatever internal thoughts she had going on and looked up quizzically. "What did you say?" she queried.

"Has your father ever mentioned the name Larchmont? Or has Saul, for that matter?"

She seemed to tumble the name through her brain a few times before shaking her head. "It doesn't ring any bells. Should it?"

Kildare shrugged. "I'm not sure. I might have found something in your father's study. It might not mean anything, but I found the name was scribbled in his notebook."

"You mean it may be a clue to finding my father?" she suddenly leaped to her feet animatedly. She grabbed Kildare's hand imploringly.

"It's possible," he replied. Kildare paused a moment before he continued, frowning. "There's more. That same sheet of paper also had another name on it. Yours."

The look of surprise on Elaine's face was genuine and Kildare knew she was just as much in the dark as he was. So much for getting anything from her, he thought. Kildare was not any closer to unraveling the mystery than he was when he followed Mullaney to Elaine's apartment. He realized it was time to take a more direct approach.

It was time for Killdevil to get to work.

◉◉◉

Vernon Lippman, otherwise known to the rest of the underworld as Vermin, was a low-level stooge in Saul's organization. He was a fence and informant who was so far down the totem pole, he was nearly an afterthought. But he had a knack of knowing just enough information to stay on Saul's payroll. That made him a person of interest for Killdevil.

The former hitman found the flunky in one of his usual hangouts, a greasy spoon in the harbor district called Candy Cane's. The place was even worse than Killdevil remembered it, the smell of stale tobacco, sweat and grease turned his stomach as he walked in the door. With a glance Killdevil saw Vernon sitting at the far end of the counter, nearest the kitchen door. Vernon looked up as the hitman sauntered in his direction, a look of shock covered the weasel's face. Before Killdevil could take more than a couple of steps, Vermin bolted towards the back door.

Killdevil raced after him, nearly knocking over a waitress overladen with platters full of sandwiches and fries in the process. Ignoring her gasp, he caught up with the stooge just as the small man reached the doorway which led to the back alley. He gave the fence a hard shove through the door and slammed him hard against a dumpster.

"Why were you running, Vermin? Do you have something to hide from me?"

"Mister Kildare! I did not recognize you at first. I didn't know you was back in town," he stammered.

"Shut your mouth, Vermin. You know why I'm back in town. You know who I'm after."

"Sure, sure. Everyone knows you have a mad on for Saul. Honestly, I don't blame you. What he did to your lady friend and all."

Killdevil glowered at the weasel, his grip tightening on the man's shirt front. "Listen closely, stooge. Congressman Fitzgerald. Saul nabbed him. Where is he?" He shoved the man harder into the side of the dumpster for emphasis.

"I–I don't know," the man stammered. "Honest. I have not heard anything about it. I'm not exactly in Saul's inner circle, you understand."

Killdevil narrowed his eyes slightly. "I don't believe you, Vermin. You have your ears to the ground on everything. What is going on between Saul and the Congressman? Spill it!"

Vermin shook his head vehemently. "Honest. I don't know. Saul is being very tight-lipped about it. Only a few of his closest boys knows anything! Maybe find Claudio. He may know a thing or two!"

"What do you know about a man named Larchmont?" Killdevil continued, ignoring Vermin's previous response.

"N–Nuthin.' I–I swear," Vermin whimpered.

The sound of the back door opening drew Killdevil's attention over his shoulder. The former hitman took one glance in that direction and saw the slack-jawed face of a youth in a cook's apron. Upon taking one look at Killdevil, the cook slammed the door shut and Kildare heard the distinct sound of a lock being turned. He returned his attention back to the hood once more, but by the look in Vermin's eyes it was someone else looking back at him. He sneered.

"Get out of my face, dammit. After the last stunt you pulled I do not have time for your games!"

"Oh come on, Stephen. Are you going to hold a grudge against me? We make such beautiful music together, you and I."

"What do you want? Just tell me and get out of my face," Killdevil bristled as he continued to hold "Vermin" against the dumpster.

"Don't be so rude, Stephen. Remember, it is you who works for me, not the other way around. Still, I feel I may have been a bit over the top during our previous conversation. I want to make amends. So why don't you off this loser and let's sign our peace treaty. Shall we?"

Killdevil furrowed his brow. "I am not going to kill Vermin. He doesn't know anything. Besides, I think he is going to send a message to Saul for me. He's going to tell him that I am coming for him, and I am going to bring hell with me!"

"Oh that is such sweet music to my ears," the not-Vermin laughed.

A moment later, Killdevil was alone in the alley once more with a very scared Vernon Lippman. He repeated the message he had recently told his erstwhile "employer" for Vermin's ears. Moments later he was back in his roadster in search of bigger game.

◉◉◉

Stephen was growing increasingly frustrated. After his interrogation of Vernon Lippman, he had made several more visits to some of Saul's lower-level stooges and so far all he got out of it was dead ends and deader bodies. Nobody knew anything about the Congressman's whereabouts, nor did they know anything about a man named Larchmont. What was the connection?

For that matter, Stephen was not even sure that the names scribbled on the notebook were even connected at all. But Larchmont's name was there just as Elaine's was, and she had no clue who he was either. It could just be coincidence, but he wasn't buying it. There had to be something more to this and someone had to know the answer he was searching for.

As Kildare sped on to his next destination his mind began to wander a bit more on Elaine. She seemed innocent of the whole matter, yet why would the Congressman arrange a marriage between her and a known mob boss? What was there to gain? Was she as innocent as she led on? Or was she somehow involved in Saul's affairs? But then why would he want her knocked off? None of it made any sense whatsoever.

No, she couldn't be involved. He could not rationalize that the pretty girl was mixed up with Saul in any way. His mind began to play tricks on him; it began to compare Elaine Franchetti to another woman who was taken from him very recently.

Lauren Dennis.

Kildare caught himself. Where did that come from? Sure, the Congressman's daughter was an attractive lady; he had noticed that the first moment he laid eyes on her at her apartment. But why would he think of her in the same way he thought of his dear departed love? After all, she was married to his mortal enemy. And he still loved Lauren.

"Get a grip on yourself, dammit!" he muttered to himself. "The Devil is messing with your head. That's all. He put the seed there. The damned fool!"

Kildare's jaw clenched as he stepped a little harder on the accelerator. He was getting tired of the game and needed to put an end to the business and find out some answers—one way or another.

◎◎◎

Saul Franchetti was not a happy man. Not that he was known for being all warm and fuzzy at the best of times. But now, he was a vessel of barely controlled rage. The news had been coming from all over that Stephen Kildare was asking a lot of questions and putting a lot of his men in the hospital—or the morgue. At least four men were found full of holes with those stupid masks covering their faces. He was fed up with these childish antics.

"Killdevil!" he spewed. "Send out every gun we got. I don't care if the streets run red with blood. Just find that man and put a bullet in him. Nobody is going to rest around here until he's buried in a pine box!"

"Yes, boss!" Sammy Moretti nodded vigorously. "Don't worry boss, we'll get him!"

Franchetti glowered. "You had better! If not, I will put you in that pine box instead!"

Franchetti waited until Moretti had left before he turned his attention to the other person in the room. The man was thin as a razor blade, with a pair of dark, intelligent eyes, and he had an extra layer of grease keeping his black hair in immaculate position. He had the aura of a cagey predator. Despite his smaller frame he carried the presence of a heavyweight prizefighter. He was truly a dangerous man. His name was Sidney Cartier, though he was known to most of the underworld simply as the Bone Carver.

"Is our honored guest all comfortable?" Saul asked the man.

A predatory smile creased one side of Sidney's mouth slightly. "Oh yes. He won't be going anywhere anytime soon."

Saul allowed a smile of his own to show on his face briefly. "Good. Then

I want you to take four men. Four of our hardest men and sit on him. I don't want Kildare to get within a hundred yards of him. Do whatever it takes. Even if you have to kill our guest. Understand?"

The Bone Carver grinned wickedly. "Oh yes. I understand all right. It will be my pleasure!"

◉◉◉

Elaine paced around the smallish safehouse like a caged tiger. She hated sitting still while her father was missing, presumably kidnapped by her husband. Considering he just tried to kill her, who knew what was happening to him. She could not believe the mess her life had turned in just the span of a matter of hours. All of it by men. Her father, the Congressman, who had arranged for her to marry that beast of a man, Saul Franchetti. Saul, for trying to have someone kill her for some unknown reason. The would-be killer, though she can't hold anything against him, for he is the one who ended up in a body bag. And then Stephen Kildare who is off doing God-knows-what to God-knows-whom, while telling her to sit on her heels. She was sick and tired of being some sort of kept woman. Left alone to rot by one or another, all the while the menfolk play their stupid games.

Well, she was not having it. Not anymore.

But what could she do? There was no phone in the safehouse, so she could not make any calls. She considered going to the local police station, but then she remembered Stephen's warning that she could not even trust the cops. But she could not stay here and wait around either.

Then a moment of inspiration hit her. Uncle Jack. Uncle Jack would know what to do. They used to be very close, though she had not seen him for a couple of years now. She was pretty sure she knew where to find him. He was a private investigator and still had an office downtown. He was sure to help her. After all, who better to turn to for a missing person than a private eye? Especially if that person was their own brother?

Elaine grabbed a coat and her purse and headed for the door. If she was lucky, she would make it cross town before he closed shop for the evening.

She just hoped he would be in.

◉◉◉

Topper Moran gazed down upon the small, affluent crowd which mingled below his feet. He saw a couple of politicians, a retired army colonel, two attorneys and one well-known banker. All of them had enough money to buy and sell anything or anyone they wanted—several times over no doubt. He sneered at the money barons.

Dante's Inferno was one of Saul's finest establishments. It was a gentleman's club which had a rather exclusive clientele. It was where all of Franchetti's biggest deals went down. So while most of the teams were out scouring the streets in search of Kildare, Topper and his men were stuck here babysitting a bunch of spoiled rich men. Topper had tried to plead his case to the big man. He tried to convince Saul that the job was better suited to Danno or Freddie Four Fingers, but Saul wasn't having it. He even tried to sweet talk Topper by saying he needed the best for this job. Moran didn't buy it for a second. But what the boss says goes and here he was staring down at all the riches of the city—and it was all off limits. It made him sick.

Saul took one more look around the large room below and saw three of his men were at their stations keeping watch. He knew there were two others down there, hidden and out of sight. He exchanged a glance with his lieutenant, Rafferty, and knew that all was quiet. Not that he would expect any less. The only one foolish enough to hit the Inferno was Killdevil, and last he heard the psychopath was targeting the lowest of the low in the organization.

There's no way he would try to tackle such a high-profile place as this. Moran was dying to know what was going on and decided it was time to make a couple of phone calls to pass the boredom.

Moran turned to the small, but opulent, office which he commandeered on the upper floor of the club. It was a perfect spot for him to oversee his operation, as it afforded a great view of the lower level, including the main entryway up front. There was a back entrance, but he had four men stationed there and any sort of attack from that direction was certain to alert him long before anyone could breach the inner bowels of the gentleman's club.

He took two steps into the office when all hell broke loose.

⊙⊙⊙

Roughing up or even killing a few of the worms at the bottom of the food chain was not making a huge impact on Saul's day to day operations and Kildare knew it. But it did serve to shake up the Franchetti organization and keep everyone on their toes. But it was time to step things up a bit and really hit his former boss where it hurt most—in the pocketbook.

Dante's Inferno was one of the biggest gentlemen's clubs in the city and at any given time there would be dozens of the richest men in town hanging out. Deals were brokered, lives and livelihoods were put on the line at the single stroke of a pen. It was Saul's golden goose.

It was time to serve the goose on a platter.

Kildare went through his options. He could try to go through the back, but he knew there would be goons stationed back there. No, he decided upon the direct approach. Kildare pulled his roadster directly in front of the club, in an area reserved for dropping off and picking up dignitaries. The door man moved forward to intercept him.

"I'm sorry sir, but you cannot park there. That is a restricted zone. Please move your car around the corner—" the door man's voice trailed off as he saw the look on Kildare's face—a look of stark hostility. He stood with his mouth agape as the man marched towards the front door. Kildare barely glanced at the man as he brushed passed him. He had sized him up as mere flunky and not a hardened man. He would pose no threat.

Kildare went over the layout of the place in his mind. While he had only been at the club on a couple of occasions while working for Saul, he knew that there was a front foyer with a small coatroom to the side. The double doors, which opened into the main room would be right in front of the foyer. A stairwell on the left wrapped around to the upper floor where a balcony and offices overlooked the main ballroom. Various doors around the room opened to small private rooms where various deals were made and where the rich and powerful could engage in other, more discreet activities. There would also be a doorway which led to the private rear entrance and Kildare knew there was a secret exit as well. One that only a select few knew about. It was originally built for the prohibition era when the club was an illegal speakeasy, but it worked well when one of the important people had to beat a hasty retreat without being seen. Stephen made a mental note of the layout and anticipated the most likely places where gunmen would be stationed. He knew he was going to be walking into a crossfire, but he hoped the club had enough patrons to cause a bit of chaos, which would work well to his favor.

Kildare drew his firearm and knocked on the front door with the butt of his pistol. A moment later, a small window opened on the heavy door and a hardened face with graying temples appeared before him.

"I'm sorry sir, but this is a private club—" for the second time in a matter of seconds Kildare silenced someone with a glare. Though the gun that was aimed at the man's face certainly helped the man lose his interest in speech.

"Everyone around here is sorry it seems. Now tell me friend, are we going to do this the easy way or the hard way?"

For his credit, the man at the door did not panic. He slammed the metal lid of the window shut before Killdevil could pull the trigger.

"The hard way it is then," Killdevil muttered as he took a couple steps back. He lunged forward with the sole of his heavy shoe striking the heavy door just right. It was a move he had used on many doors in the past, just none so strong as the one he was trying to use it on now. He heard a satisfying crack of hard wood, but the door didn't shatter as he had hoped. He took another step back and threw his shoulder at it, this time the door flew apart. Killdevil let the momentum carry him through the doorway and low, where he landed low to the floor, a pair of bullets screaming over his head. He had landed off to the right near the coatroom and rolled to a knee. He was able to take in the scene briefly. The man who greeted him at the door was lying on the floor beneath the ruins of the shattered door. A large splinter of wood had pierced the man in the calf, and he was howling in pain. Next to him stood two gunmen who were trying to draw a bead on him. They would not get another opportunity to fire again. A pair of shots from Killdevil's pistol caught both thugs in the chest and put them out of the fight for good. He considered putting another round in the injured man lying by the door but could tell by the way he was lying that the door did more damage to him than he at first thought. He would not cause any more trouble. There were bigger fish to fry on the other side of the twin foyer doors.

Killdevil knew the gunshots were most likely heard by the club's patrons and that panic was probably already starting to set in amongst the high and mighty. Good. That was what he wanted. He drew his second pistol just as the double doors began to open.

Two thugs came out firing. Killdevil plugged the one on the left with a shot in the face—putting him out of the fighting immediately, but he had to leap to the side to avoid the other gunman's fire. He pulled off a couple of quick shots and one buried itself in the man's shoulder, knocking him to the floor. Moments later, chaos ensued as some patrons came pouring out, running past both Killdevil and the unlucky mook who was still pinned under the front door. He shrieked in pain as he was trampled by the panicked mob.

Killdevil fought against the streaming horde like a salmon going upriver. He managed to make the main ballroom in the mass confusion without being shot at by any other gunmen, but once he was inside he was in the open once more. Realizing his predicament, he dove behind a heavy oaken

Two thugs came out firing.

table just as several shots began to pepper the area he had been standing in moments earlier.

He was safe for the moment, but the shots had come from at least three different directions, and he was caught in a bad crossfire. He could not defend his position for long as the enemy had him surrounded. A couple of the rounds had come from above, indicating they commanded the high ground as well. He had to do something quick, or his crusade was going to come to a sudden and definite end. Fortunately, he did not come unprepared. He reached into the pocket of his suit coat and pulled out a few small round objects. Each of the balls had a small wick sticking out. Killdevil pulled out his lighter from his breast pocket and lit the first ball, tossing it over to his right. He repeated the action with the other two balls, sending them in other directions until they formed a small triangle around his position. Immediately, the room filled up with a cloud of thick, black smoke. His eyes began to tear up, and he grabbed his handkerchief, tying it around his face. After a count of five, Killdevil was up and moving.

He began to run in a zig zag pattern towards the direction he knew one of the gunmen was sitting. He heard someone coughing and cursing and soon he could see the shadowy silhouette of a man in the smoke. Waiting briefly to make sure he was facing a mafia goon and not some senator or industrialist, Killdevil drew his knife. By the time the thug knew that the hitman was there, it was too late. One thug down, but Killdevil had no idea how many more were lurking in the smoky room.

He went on the hunt.

It was slow going as Killdevil had to make his way through the roiling smoke, all the while trying to dodge the random bullets which continued to fly. The hitmen on top of the stairs continued to take pot shots into the cloud of smoke—some of which were getting quite close. At one point, Killdevil heard a man nearby grunt, the thug taking an unfortunate bullet from friendly fire. Killdevil dispatched two other thugs, but knew he was running short on time, for someone had to have raised the alarm by now. He made a beeline for the area he knew the stairs to be. He only hoped the smoke would hold out long enough to get him most of the way up the stairs before being seen.

Killdevil stumbled when his foot struck the first step, but he caught himself against the banister. He held off a curse, holding his breath waiting for gunshots to rain down on his position. After a pregnant pause, he realized the sound must not have traveled far. The hitman let out a sigh of relief as he made his way up the staircase. His luck ran out while he was halfway up the steps as the smoke cloud began to dissipate. He was about to be a sitting duck, so he did the only thing he could do—he charged!

One thug stood at the top of the stairwell, his eyes and gun were both pointed down towards the ballroom, which was probably a saving grace for Killdevil. By the time the goon caught the movement in the corner of his eye and began to shift his aim, Killdevil was on top of him. His pistol barking out a pair of deadly coughs which caught the man in the chest. Before he had a chance to fall, Killdevil caught the dead man and held him in front of him as two other hitmen turned in his direction. His meat shield danced as a trio of bullets struck the thug's body. Killdevil fired back from under the corpse's arm and heard the satisfying sound of a man crying out in pain. More bullets reached out for him, and he dropped the thug and rolled into a nearby office, wincing as he felt one of the bullets graze his left calf.

He had rolled right into the barrel of Topper Moran's waiting pistol. Topper's wicked grin was outlined above the deadly hand cannon.

⊚⊚⊚

Elaine entered the nondescript building and found her uncle's office on the second floor. She had lucked out and found Jack Fitzgerald just as he was locking up for the evening. He took one look at her and immediately unlocked the door and ushered her in. The outer waiting room was small, with one small desk and a couple of chairs. A small table sat in between them. He offered her a seat and took the chair next to her.

"What is wrong, El?" he asked her with a look of great concern etched on his face.

"I'm worried about dad. You had to hear about the dreadful attack and his disappearance—" Elaine's voice trailed off in an outbreak of sobs as the recent events bubbled over.

Jack Fitzgerald nodded his head. "Yes, of course I did. It is a major news story, and as much as he and I never really got along very well, he is still my brother. I have taken a vested interest in this and will do all that I can to make sure you and your father are reunited." He paused and handed Elaine his handkerchief. "I had spoken with him the other day, and he was very concerned about something. He confided in me a little about it, and I may have a lead in which to find him. But I might need a little help from you. If you don't mind, of course."

Elaine, empowered by the possibility of a lead, managed to compose herself once more. "Yes of course, I would do anything to help find him.

Just tell me what you need me to do, and I will do it."

Jack smiled faintly. "That's my El. I was hoping you would say that. Now then, this is what we're going to do—"

◉◉◉

Killdevil was a dead man. The look on Moran's face told him as much. And even if Moran would miss at point-blank range, which was highly unlikely, there were still several more thugs charging down the hallway who would be in the room within seconds. The former mob man was in as tight a fix as he had ever been in. Even though he was trapped, he still had his wits about him, and he was known for his quick thinking when he needed to. He also knew Moran personally, having worked with him a time or two during his days as one of Saul's hitmen.

He heard footsteps and caught movement out of the corner of his eye. The thugs have gotten their bravado up and were perched just outside the doorway. He held up his hands as if in surrender and slowly got to his knees. "All right, Moran. Looks like you got me. Now what are you going to do with me?"

"Ahh Stephen. It looks like I am about to get some long-awaited revenge for Paulie Angelli is what I am about to do," Moran replied gleefully. "Now stand up, so I can put you back down permanently. I would hate to do you on your knees, but if that is the way you want to go out, then who am I to overlook your last request."

Kildare thought quickly. "You certainly could do that, Topper. You got me dead to rights. But if I were you I would think about the big picture."

Moran's grin soured. "What big picture, Kildare? What are you trying to say?"

"Aw, ignore him and plug him, boss. He's just messing with you," one of Moran's men called out from the doorway.

"Yeah, finish him," another goon added. "He wasted half the crew. Let him have it!"

Killdevil saw the scowl on Moran's face harden. His time was just about up. He slowly stood and turned to face Moran straight on, as if to indicate the other men meant nothing. He was taking a bit of a risk by putting a nest of vipers to his back, but he hoped the little subtlety would feed Topper's ego. "Think about it Topper. You shoot me down now and get revenge for Paulie and your men and that's great. But then what? Life goes on and you are still in the same place you are now. But if you hand me over to Saul alive, why then you would be number one in his eyes. The sky would be the limit for you. The choice is yours, Topper. A bit of revenge now or do you play it cool and join the next tax bracket? Think about it."

There was a long tense pause as Moran thought about the prospect. Perspiration began to trickle off his forehead as the wheels spun in his head. He banged the gun lightly against his head a couple times in frustration before turning to the thugs in the doorway. "Gustavo, get the car around. Halsey, keep your rod trained on our boy here and if he so much as blinks too hard, waste him. We're going to go talk to the big man." He turned and faced Kildare; his eyes filled with venomous hatred. "You think you may have bought yourself some freedom, but all you did was buy yourself some long, agonizing pain. You are a traitor to our Family, and I can't wait to watch what Saul does to you for all that you did to us. You're still going to die Stephen. It's just going to take you a long, long time."

◉◉◉

Kildare had been stripped down, blindfolded, and bound hand and foot before being unceremoniously dumped in the trunk of one of Moran's cars. He heard distant sirens as the vehicle tore away from the gentleman's club; no doubt the cops were finally on their way to investigate the chaos which had broken out at the Inferno. It had seemed like hours since his brazen attack on the club, but it had all taken just a matter of minutes. Stephen was trying to be cognizant of what direction they were heading, but whoever was driving was playing it smart and began to take numerous turns on what proved to be a winding and circuitous route meant to disorient him. Finally, Kildare had given up his attempts and concentrated on trying to figure out a way out of his current predicament.

Stephen was no good to Elaine if he was dead, he thought morbidly. He tried to free himself from his bonds, but the thug who hogtied him was a professional, and he could barely move his hands or feet. He was on his side and tried to push off with one shoulder and try to budge the trunk lid with the other, but that likewise had no effect other than to jostle him around. He was in a fix all right and at last decided to conserve his strength and bide his time to a more opportune time to escape.

He just hoped that an opportunity presented itself.

◉◉◉

Once more Sully Venkman had gone in to face his hot-tempered boss, though this time he hoped the news he would present Saul Franchetti would be more to the big man's liking. The fact that Saul was on the phone and in relatively good spirits was another mark in his favor. Saul waved him in but held a finger up. Venkman halted just inside the doorway and waited his turn, far be it from him to spoil the boss' rare, good mood. Sully saw the slim and silent frame of Sidney Cartier, the Bone Carver, standing silently in one corner of the room. Cartier was staring at Sully with a smug look on his face. Venkman felt some cold perspiration on his face, for the Bone Carver was a scary individual, and he hated being in the killer's presence.

Shortly afterwards the phone conversation wound down and Franchetti hung up the receiver. He let his under boss stew for a minute before looking up and addressing the intruder. "What is it, Venkman? I thought you were busy looking for Elaine. Do you have some sort of mind-blowing information for me about my lovely wife?"

Sully was not sure if Saul was being facetious with him or not, for the tone in Franchetti's voice hinted that the mob boss knew something. Either the boss was testing Sully, or he was having some sort of fun with him. Either way, Sully knew Saul was a powder keg at the best of times. "I am sorry to say, boss, that I have no new leads towards your wife, but I do come with some other news that you might be interested in.

Saul cocked his head at Sully's revelation slightly, though a touch of impatience betrayed his outwardly mild temperament. "Well, I don't have all day, Sully. What is it?"

Sully swallowed back his nerves, for he knew he was still on thin ice with the imposing mob boss. "Well I just heard that Topper Moran is on his way here now. He's caught Kildare, and he is bringing him here all gift-wrapped like."

Franchetti mused over the news a moment before replying. He walked over to Sully and clapped the man on the back. "That is terrific news Sully. Terrific indeed. But I need you to get a word out to Topper. Tell him to hold off on bringing him here. Have Topper put him on ice at the garage until he hears otherwise. I want you to go there and see to it personally." Saul glanced at Sidney for a moment before continuing. "Sid and I have some other business to attend to. It seems that not everyone in the organization is totally incompetent." The last bit was said with barely disguised malice.

Sully was uncertain what Saul was hinting at, but when he saw the vicious smile which was plastered on Sidney's face, he felt his blood drain.

He had the distinct feeling that the ice he was standing on was beginning to crack.

◉◉◉

Topper Moran was sitting at the desk in the tiny office of the garage, fuming. It was a far cry from the palatial office he was sitting in a mere couple of hours earlier. He captured Saul's number one thorn, the almighty Stephen Kildare, and instead of rubbing shoulders with Saul he was stuck here in an auto garage, babysitting the schmuck. On top of that, Saul saw fit to put that nobody Sully in charge of *his* operation. Moran glared contemptuously at the simpering fool, who was nervously standing near the garage doorway. "One of these days, Venkman, you and I are going to have some words," Moran muttered under his breath. "You can count on it."

Besides Venkman and himself, Moran had the three remaining members of his crew with him. The rest were sitting on cold slabs or nursing their wounds from the attack on the Inferno. Five of his men were dead, and four more were too messed up to be of any good. Moran considered offing the punk Kildare now, but he knew that would be suicide now that Franchetti was aware of the traitor's capture. Topper cursed again as he paced the tiny office like a caged tiger. He did the only thing he could do; he began to take his anger out on the sparse furnishings. He hefted the tiny chair in the room and slammed it against the wall.

◉◉◉

Sully leaned against the wall and kept watch out the side door of the garage. He knew his days were numbered, though he was not certain what the final straw had been. Saul seemed awfully smug during the last meeting—he knew something, and Sully did not like it. Then there was the Bone Carver. The man was dangerous and loved killing a bit too much for Venkman's liking. The man was a Grade A psychopath, and he did not care who he killed. Sully knew he was on borrowed time, and he was running scared. He glanced back at the small office after he heard a crash in that direction. Topper Moran was a hothead, and he knew the man wanted to rise in the organization any way he could. In his current mood, Sully did not trust the man to be rational. Venkman felt like he was alone. One did not live long in this line of work on your own. What he needed was an ally.

He turned and looked at the small card table which was set up in the middle of the floor where the three surviving gunmen were sitting, One of them, Woody, had a bandage wrapped on his head and another, Gustavo, had his left arm in a sling. They were passing the time playing cards waiting expectantly for their grand rewards for turning in the infamous Stephen Kildare.

The man of question was tied up on a chair along a nearby wall. The surrounding area had been carefully cleared away and his bindings had been tightened to make sure he would not be able to free himself.

Venkman took the scene in and slowly a plan began to evolve.

◉◉◉

Elaine was so lost in thought that she barely noticed the buildings which whipped past the window as Jack raced through town. She was excited for the possibility she would soon be reunited with her father, though there was something nagging her, and she could not figure out what that was.

Jack noticed the sideways look that Elaine was giving him and glanced over at her. "Are you going to keep staring at me or are you going to ask the question that seems to be weighing on your mind?"

Jack's sudden outburst startled Elaine after the lengthy silence inside the car. "Uh, well. I was wondering when you spoke with father last?"

"Is that all? It was the night before last. It was around dinner time, I should think. He seemed distressed and needed to unburden himself upon me. What kind of brother would I be if I didn't lend an ear?"

Elaine stifled a gasp as she realized it was not Saul who her father had spoken to in his study that evening, but her uncle. Jack smirked as he slowly opened one side of his coat to reveal the butt of his pistol, just enough for Elaine to cop a good look.

"Now don't get any funny ideas. Just stay calm and peaceful like," he said to her in the same gentlemanly manner he had always used with her. "I like you kiddo, I really do, and I don't want to see no harm come to you. But business is business, understand?"

Elaine shrunk back against the car door and stared in horror at her uncle. "How—how could you? Your own brother, your own family—" she began to sob.

"Yes he is my family, but you don't get it, doll. He is the one that turned on us—on me. Your father was no saint. He was up to his teeth with Saul's business. But then his feet got cold. Real cold. So I tried to reason with him, but he refused to listen to the big picture. As I said, it is just business."

Elaine continued to sob quietly as she took everything in. She could scarcely believe it, yet she wasn't naïve, and she did hear the rumors. Could it be true? She tried to clear her head. She willed the sobs away and began to look outside realizing there were fewer buildings flashing by now. They had driven quite a way, and she saw they were at the outskirts of town and heading for the waterfront. "Where are you taking me?" she queried uneasily.

Uncle Jack smirked again. "I told you; I am reuniting you with your father. As I said, I had a job for you to do. Or should I say that Saul has one."

"Job? What job?"

This time Jack chuckled, and his voice changed subtly. No longer the sweet and genuine voice of her Uncle Jack, this was the voice of pure evil. "Simple. You're going to kill Congressman Fitzgerald."

◎◎◎

Venkman wandered over to Stephen Kildare with a swagger and a glower. "You think you are a tough guy, well in my book you ain't nothin' but a two-bit gun in a fifty-cent suit." He punctuated the unflattering remark with a hard slap to Kildare's face, which drew a small trickle of blood and a round of laughter from the three mooks at the card table. The blow was strong enough to knock Kildare's chair over.

Sully reached down and up righted the chair, showing a surprising amount of strength as he continued to jaw at the prisoner. He continued his little tirade on Killdevil until Topper Moran poked his head out to see what the commotion was. "Hey, settle down out there and leave 'im alone. Saul will do him in soon enough!" he shouted before turning back and walking back into the tiny office.

"Screw you, Topper. I call the shots here," Sully responded halfheartedly. "Aww, nuts," he muttered as he turned away from Kildare and walked over to the table where the thugs were sitting. "C'mon boys, let's play some cards."

Stephen Kildare took the whole incident in stoically. Sully and he had never seen eye to eye, but he was rather surprised by the man's sudden outburst. He was even more surprised when the under boss slid something into his hand surreptitiously while he was straightening the chair.

Despite his predicament, Killdevil could not help but smile when he realized that the item he was holding was a knife. His hands were bound behind his back, so it was not easy to manipulate the blade against the ropes, but he began to work on the bindings as best he could. He winced a couple of times as he nicked himself on the sharp edge. Killdevil kept one eye on the poker game where Venkman sat with the three thugs, actively ignoring the bound prisoner.

Stephen continued to work while he sized up Venkman. He was baffled as to what the man's motives were, but he was not about to look a gift horse in the mouth.

He had just gotten one of his hands free when the shouting began.

◉◉◉

"Wh—what did you just say?"

Jack flashed a wicked smile at his niece. "I said you were going to kill the Congressman."

Elaine shook her head defiantly. "You expect me to kill—kill my own father? Your brother?"

Jack's smile faded. "Look. I don't want him dead any more than you do. But he grew soft, and now he is a liability to Saul. So he must be silenced."

"But, why me?"

Jack glanced at Elaine, and she caught a trace of sadness on his face, though it quickly vanished. "It's simple. You know too much of the situation. Frankly, you are a liability too. The only way Saul is going to let you live is if you become an accomplice. Don't you see? It's the only way I could convince him to let you live. We're family, you and me. We gotta stick together."

Elaine was horrified. She tried to rationalize that the monster in front of her was still her Uncle Jack, but her mind could not fathom it. "You're mad!" she screamed. "Mad if you think I would do such a horrible thing!" Before Jack could react, Elaine flung open the car door and vanished into the night air.

"Stupid bitch!" Jack snarled as he slammed on the brakes. He pounded his fist on the steering wheel once before he slid out of the car. He found Elaine lying on the side of the road, unmoving. He got close to her and nudged her a couple times to make sure she was not faking unconsciousness. She had a small knot on her head and a few scrapes on her body from the awkward landing but otherwise she seemed to have survived the failed escape attempt little worse for the wear. Not that it would do her much good, he thought. He picked up her limp form and carried her to the car where he unceremoniously dumped her in the back seat. "Stupid, stupid bitch," he mumbled. "Now we have to do it the hard way."

◎◎◎

"You cheated, you scumbag! I saw you pull that Jack from the bottom of the deck, you no good cheatin' bum," the thug called Halsey shouted as he tossed down his cards in disgust. He pointed his meaty finger at Venkman.

"I did no such thing. Your eyesight is as deplorable as your card playin," Venkman retorted.

Halsey rose to his feet, sending his chair flying backwards. "Deplorable? I'll show you deplorable you no good rotten fink!" Halsey threw a wild swing at Venkman that just missed the under boss, though it caught Gustavo's wounded wing as the big Italian was getting to his feet, eliciting a loud howl from the thug. By this time, the three mafia men were raising such a racket that they did not see Killdevil rise from his chair, his hands now free. Only Woody saw their prisoner leap up from his chair, but Killdevil put him down with a flash of his newly gained knife before the thug could shout a warning.

Venkman and Halsey were paired off in a struggle of fisticuffs as Gustavo tried to pull out a gun with his offhand. He had seen Woody crumple to the ground and had turned his attention towards Killdevil, but with his arm in a sling he was too slow by far. It wasn't long before he joined his partner in death, the hilt of the gleaming knife buried in his chest.

Killdevil managed to wrest Gustavo's gun from his hand as the thug fell, and he turned his attention on the fight which was still going on between the two members of Saul's empire. Just then, Sully let loose with a hard right hand that smashed against the other thug's jaw. The back of Halsey's head caught the edge of his chair as he went down and there was an audible, sickening crunch.

Venkman turned and smiled at Killdevil then, but the smile faded quickly as a gunshot echoed throughout the garage. A small red circle began to flower on Venkman's stomach as he fell over.

It was Topper.

Killdevil cursed as he dove to the side and tried to bring his appropriated gun to bear on the goon leader. He fired off a couple of quick shots as he rolled along the concrete. He caught a glimpse of Moran ducking back into the little office. Killdevil knew that the gunshots would be heard, and his time was short. He had to take Moran alive and find out who Larchmont was and where Elaine's father was being kept.

... the three mafia men did not see Killdevil rise from his chair....

Moran peeked his head out and snapped off a shot. Killdevil returned one of his own and as Moran ducked again, Stephen quickly shifted off to his right. Soon Moran poked his head up again to fire, but he was looking in the wrong direction. Killdevil fired first, the bullet taking Topper in the shoulder, sending the man sprawling.

Killdevil pounced.

Moran was ready for him however and struck out with the toe of his shoe, catching Killdevil's wrist and knocking his gun to the floor. Moran still had a lot of fight despite the bullet wound. Killdevil realized that Topper was about to have the drop on him, so he closed quickly and grabbed the hood's gun hand. The two jockeyed for position in a battle of raw power and leverage. It was a pretty even struggle, with Moran trying to turn his gun to bear on Killdevil; and for a moment it appeared as if he was going to succeed.

"Tell me, Moran! Who is Larchmont?" Killdevil spoke through gritted teeth.

Moran said nothing; his entire focus was on the power struggle as he continued to try to get his gun angled on his opponent. It seemed to work for slowly and inexorably the barrel began to point in Killdevil's direction. Killdevil reversed his hold, pulling Moran off-balance just as the crook pulled the trigger. The gun went off, but the barrel was no longer pointing at Killdevil.

Moran's eyes bugged out, and then he fell to the concrete floor, a gaping hole in his chest.

Killdevil cursed. He knelt next to Topper to try to get the information out of him, but it was too late. Topper Moran was dead. And so was Killdevil's lead on the Congressman.

Or was it?

Stephen walked back to where the card table was upended and knelt next to Sully Venkman. The under boss was in bad shape, but Killdevil heard the telltale signs of ragged breathing.

"Why'd you do it Sully?" Killdevil asked in a soft compassioned voice. "Why'd you turn on Saul?"

Venkman took a couple of ragged breaths. "The writing—was on the wall. It was just a matter—of—time. I decided—I wanted to be—on the winning team—for once."

Venkman was fading quickly and Killdevil knew he didn't have much time. "Sully. Tell me. Who is Larchmont?"

There was no response for quite some time, but then a soft chuckle escaped Sully's lips. "You got it wrong, Stevie Boy. Larchmont—is not a person—it's a place. It's in—Westchester. Go to the—pier. Saul's yacht."

Stephen cursed himself. He thought it was Elaine's name written on the sheet of paper, but it wasn't Elaine, It was Elanor. The name of Saul's yacht was the *Elanor II*. Stephen recalled hearing that Saul had bought the yacht a long time ago on a whim and had planned on refurbishing it and turning it into some sort of business venture. Nothing ever came of it, however and the yacht just sat there and collected dust, all but forgotten. This was all before Killdevil's time with the Saul organization, so he had never seen the boat firsthand.

Sully Venkman was seized with a coughing fit, and this drew Killdevil's attention back to the under boss. Sully looked at Killdevil, with serenity in his eyes. "Get Saul, Stevie Boy. Kill the son—of a—" Sully never finished the sentence, the last word died with him.

"I will Sully. You better damn believe I will."

Stephen stood up and turned to leave but paused and stared back down at the corpse of Sully Venkman and sighed.

"I know you're there. Spit it out, I don't have time for your games."

Sully's corpse chuckled. "My you are getting perceptive these days. That just means you and I are more connected than ever. That is good."

"Yeah, you wish. Now what do you want to say, I have work to do."

"Far be it from me to get in the way of your work. Trust me, that is the last thing I want to do. So go play the hero."

"I ain't no hero," Killdevil muttered.

The corpse began to giggle. "Oh but you are. You are *my* hero, after all!"

"Aww, stick it!" Killdevil growled as he stormed off. It was time to finish this once and for all, he mused. The devilish laughter which echoed behind him was quickly forgotten as he stormed out of the garage.

Stephen Kildare slid behind the wheel of Moran's car and gunned the engine. Westchester was about an hour's drive, and it would give him some time to think of what he would do when he got his hands on Saul Franchetti.

◉◉◉

The blackness slowly gave way to various shades of gray as Elaine regained consciousness. She opened her eyes and regretted it instantly as her head swam and her stomach roiled. She felt very sick, but alive. She couldn't feel her arms and legs at first and soon realized she was tied to a chair. Elaine thought she heard a familiar voice calling to her, but she couldn't focus on it at first. Finally, the cobwebs began to clear, and her vision cleared along with it. She then saw someone she never thought she would see again, staring at her with a concerned look on his face.

"D–Dad?"

"Hey Princess. Are you all right?"

"Yeah—I think so," she replied, looking around at her surroundings. They were in a tiny room, both of them tied up to chairs. She thought she felt her body swaying slightly, though she couldn't tell if that was the after-effects of the knock on her head or if it was actually happening. "Where—where are we?"

"I think we're on Saul's yacht. We are his guests, so it would seem."

"What do we do now?" Elaine asked. "How do we get out of this?"

Before the Congressman could respond, the small door to the cabin opened and three men walked into the room. Elaine glared at her Uncle Jack and then let out a savage snarl as Saul Franchetti appeared, a smug smile on his face. She did not recognize the third man. He was slender and unassuming, but there was something about him that gave her the creeps.

"I'm afraid that for the Congressman there is no getting out of this," Saul replied, as he walked over to Elaine. "But, my dearest wife, you can rejoin me at my side. No more living on your own. You can stay with me now. You will be safe and sound. All you must do is tie up one little loose end for me."

The rage and anger turned Elaine's face a dark crimson. "Never, you animal!" she shouted. "Kill me if you must, I would rather die than be married to you for one more second!" She spit at Saul in a final act of defiance.

The smirk faded on Saul's face as he withdrew a handkerchief from his breast pocket and wiped the gob of saliva from his cheek. He balled up his handkerchief and flung it back at her. "Pity. I was hoping you would be more reasonable. Ah well, I am sure I will get used to bachelor life again." He glanced at the creepy man at his side. "As we agreed, Sidney. She is all yours."

The creepy man withdrew a long blade from nowhere and grinned as he took a step closer to the helpless woman.

Elaine felt the panic set in as she cast her eyes around the room. Her father was struggling with his bonds, trying to get free. She gazed imploringly at her uncle, but he looked away from her then, and she knew he would not be of any help.

"You can't do that to her, you monster!" her father shouted as he redoubled his efforts to break loose. He was animated with rage and desperation and then suddenly he was free. He leaped up and moved to intercept the bloodthirsty killer when a gunshot went off. Congressman Fitzgerald grasped his shoulder and fell to the floor.

The smoke was still seeping out of the barrel of Jack's gun.

Elaine was horrified. Her uncle just shot her father in cold blood. She stared at the man she had known her entire life, though now she realized she never really knew him at all.

In the back of her mind, she was aware that the creep with the knife was behind her, but she no longer cared. Her life just fell apart in front of her eyes.

The shock began to set in, and she barely registered the shouting and gunshots which seemed to burst out all around her.

◉◉◉

It was child's play for Stephen Kildare to break into the records room of the yacht club and find out the berth number for the *Elanor II*. It was on a pier at the far end of the harbor, and it did not take long for him to locate the boat. It was at the end of the wide-open pier and there were not many other boats in the area. He saw several men, walking around on the boat. He knew they would be keeping a watchful eye. The hard part was going to be getting to the ship unseen.

He began to strip down until he was down to his shorts. He cast a glance at the rod he had taken from Moran's crew but left it with the pile of clothes on the ground. It would do him no good now. But he still had the knife that Venkman gave him. He gripped it firmly, it felt comfortable in his hand.

Killdevil made his way to the pier and slipped into the water, within seconds he was beneath the surface and all but invisible to the ship. He swam out to the yacht and slipped his head out of the water to get his bearings. He was near the aft of the boat. The hitman smiled at his fortune for there was a ladder very near at hand. He would not have to shimmy a rope to get onboard. He began to climb.

Killdevil's luck did not last, however. He was only a few steps up the ladder when he heard footsteps above. He stopped his climb and held his breath. Someone was standing just above him. He heard the telltale signs of a lighter being flicked and saw a brief flash of light. The faint scent of tobacco wafted in his direction. A moment later he heard footsteps again, but they were fading away.

Killdevil resumed climbing and got to the top just as a gunshot rang out. He ducked down instinctively before realizing that the shot was muffled and not directed at him. It came from below deck. He had hoped to take out as many of Saul's men as possible before going down there, but all bets were off, and his plans evaporated completely when there was a shout behind him. He had been spotted.

Killdevil dived to his right and threw his knife in one smooth motion. The blade caught the gunman in the throat. Another man came running out at him from the front of the ship, but Killdevil met him head on and used the other man's momentum to flip him up and over, where he landed with a splash in the water below. A third thug was standing nearby, drawing a bead on him, but Killdevil snatched a boat hook and slammed it against the man's gun hand, sending the gun flying. His backswing caught the thug on the side of his head and put him out of action.

By now the rest of the gunmen had his location down and bullets began to fly all around him. He ducked behind a bench which housed some life preservers. Killdevil looked around desperately. Stephen was outgunned and armed only with a hook pole. He could not afford to be pinned down. He needed a distraction. Kildare saw a small gas can near his feet and kicked it lightly. It sloshed. A grim smile crossed his face. It was risky but it was the only play he had. He caught the lip of the handle with his hook pole and hurled the gas can as far as he could. It slammed down on the deck on the far side.

Shots rang out as the gunmen drew fire upon the sudden noise. A bullet ricocheted off the gas can and caused a spark. Immediately, the spilled gas burst into a fireball of flame. A man covered in flames screamed as he toppled over the edge of the boat into the water below. The other two men quickly fled as the flames began to spread across the ship.

Killdevil was nearly out of time, the fire would engulf the entire boat in short order. He raced to the doorway which he knew had to lead to the cabin below. If the Congressman was down there he had to free him. And if Saul was there, he would have to be dealt with too.

He did not expect to find Elaine there as well.

He flung open the cabin door and took the scene in with one glance. Elaine was there tied up to a chair, staring at the limp body of the Congressman. There were three others in the room. One man whom he did not recognize held a gun on Elaine. Killdevil took him to be one of Saul's cronies. The biggest danger by far, however, was Sidney Cartier. The Bone Carver had a knife out and was inches away from Elaine, looking to live up to his nickname. Then there was Saul. The mafia boss was the one nearest the door and stood between Killdevil and Cartier.

Saul had turned around when Killdevil busted in. He too had a gun in his hand, and he was tracking it in Killdevil's direction. The deadly hitman knew that Saul was not known for his gun play, usually allowing others to do the killing for him, so he was not too concerned. He grabbed the man's wrist in a steel grip as he delivered a backhand which caught the mob boss in the temple. Gun, and man both went flying.

Killdevil glanced briefly back at the other man with a gun, but the man seemed content to keep it directed at Elaine and her father, who was still not moving. He turned his attention to Cartier who had likewise turned and faced him, his blade menacingly waving in front of him, a wicked gleam in his eye.

"I have been waiting for this," the Bone Carver said behind his grin. "My chance to carve up the famous Killdevil like a Christmas turkey."

"We'll see about that," Killdevil replied coolly as he shuffled a little to the side, trying to get a good position on his opponent.

The two jockeyed for position, playing a deadly game of cat and mouse for several seconds until suddenly the Bone Carver pounced. Killdevil spun around and sidestepped him. He rabbit-punched Cartier in the back and sent the man down hard. Cartier was winded but not out, so Killdevil moved in to strike again.

"Stop where you are," Jack growled.

Killdevil glanced back and saw that the other man had his gun drawn on him now. Killdevil's back was to the gunman, and he was caught leaning the wrong way. He would never reach him in time. Jack had him dead to rights. Stephen cursed himself for forgetting about the stooge in the heat of battle.

"This is it, Kildare. Time for your big exit," Jack glowered at him, a look of deathly menace.

Kildare knew Jack was not going to hesitate. He had to make a move, though he knew he would never make it in time.

A gunshot went off, but it was not Jack's gun that had fired. It was Saul's; and it was fired by Walter Fitzgerald.

Elaine screamed as her Uncle Jack's head seemed to disintegrate before her eyes, but she recovered quickly. Her father was at her side then, one arm hanging limply, he worked furiously on her bindings and quickly freeing her from the chair.

The flames had begun to reach the lower parts of the boat now and smoke was thickening in the small cabin. "Get Elaine and get out of here," Killdevil snarled. "I have to finish this." Killdevil glanced around and realized Saul was gone. He had run like a coward. Killdevil's payback would have to wait. As the Congressman and his daughter left, Killdevil returned his attention to Cartier, who was just regaining his feet.

"Ahh, a final showdown to see who goes down with the sinking ship. I like it. It has style," the Bone Carver cooed as he began to stalk Killdevil like a panther stalks his prey. But Killdevil was no simple prey, and he held his ground. He shifted himself from side to side, once more looking for an opening in which to launch his own counter strike.

He would never get the opportunity as the boat was rocked with an explosion.

The blast had blown out a good chuck of the ship's port side, but miraculously the boat did not sink immediately. Stephen Kildare lost sight of Sidney Cartier in the ensuing chaos, but it mattered little to him then. All that mattered was to escape the flames and roiling smoke and get off the doomed vessel. His arms and chest were wracked with pain, and he knew he had suffered some pretty bad burns as well as a fair number of cuts and bruises from flying shrapnel. He groped and stumbled his way until he was suddenly free-falling. A moment later he splashed into the refreshing water, and he was free. Stephen found himself floating further down the pier, a bit dazed and exhausted. He held on to the pier's support beam for a moment to catch his breath. He heard laughter above him, and then saw an arm stretched out in front of him, and above it was the grinning Congressman.

◎◎◎

EPILOGUE

Sidney Cartier floated in the water and stared at the wreckage of the *Elanor II,* flames still silhouetting it in a halo of demonic fury. He fumed inwardly but was comforted by the fact that this was not going to be the last time he crossed paths with Stephen Kildare. They would definitely be meeting again, and next time it would be the Bone Carver who comes out on top. He looked forward to cutting up the bastard and handing his head over to Saul Franchetti personally. He began to grin wickedly as a plan developed in his mind.

◎◎◎

The Congressman, his arm still in a sling, had made a few phone calls. Since his daughter's marriage was made under duress, he was able to arrange an annulment. Elaine was a free woman. He also arranged to have her moved to a secret location where she could live out her life, free from Saul's tyranny. She was not happy with the idea of having to start over somewhere else, but with both her father and Stephen Kildare reminding her it was for her best interest, she finally relented.

Walter Fitzgerald and Stephen Kildare said their farewells and then it was just Stephen and Elaine alone in the room.

Kildare gave Elaine a wan smile. "I swear that someday he will no longer be a threat to your safety. His day is coming. I guarantee that."

Elaine smiled brightly. "Somehow I believe you, Stephen. I just wish—"

Stephen gave her an inquisitive look. "You just wish what?"

Elaine sighed. "Well, If maybe I had you around—you know for protection—that maybe I could stay here."

"For protection, huh?" he responded with a twinkle in his eye.

She grinned at him. "Sure, I mean that would be one reason anyway." Her grin faded and she grew a bit more serious. "I mean, do you think you and I—if the situation was different—that we could—"

Stephen sighed. "Look, Elaine. It's complicated. You see, there's—"

"There's another. That's what you were going to say, right? I should have known—," Elaine turned away shamefacedly. "I'm such a fool!"

Stephen took a step closer and put his hands on her shoulders. "You're no fool. Yes there's another. Or rather—there was."

Elaine turned then and saw sadness in the man's eyes for the first time. "Who was she?"

Stephen's eyes met Elaine's in such a way that a spark passed through them then. A spark that could have been so much more, but in his mind he knew that it could not be. "Her name was Lauren. She's gone now. But she's with me still."

Elaine nodded her head. She understood.

Stephen gave her a kiss on the forehead. Donned his black-banded fedora and walked out the door. Part of him wanted to turn back and run into Elaine's arms. He knew she could make him happy, but he still had Lauren on his mind.

And as for his heart, well that was still hers as well.

THE END

MORE KILLDEVIL...

When I wrote the original Killdevil story for *Airship 27 Productions*, I was not sure how it would work out. This was a character I created for the purpose of including in the *Mystery Men & Women* series, and while I really liked the character concept from the beginning, I wasn't sure if I was going to like *writing* the character or not. It was also one of the longer stories I had written as my comfort zone is closer to the 8000-12,000 range. Well I needn't have worried. I LOVE writing Killdevil.

At least the first story. The question was whether or not he would be a one trick pony or if I had enough ideas to keep him busy. For that reason, while I left the story wide open for further adventures, I also made sure that it had a solid enough ending in case the well had run dry. I let him sit in the back of my mind for a while. I knew if he was going to return to the printed page, he had lots of unfinished business with his former boss, Saul. I knew I also had to keep his "other boss" in the mix as well.

I also knew there had to be a pretty dame in the mix, it is a pulpy mafia story after all, and besides being a coldhearted killer, Stephen was a romantic. From there, the story just began to write itself, much like the original. I made sure to not forget where he came from and tried my best to show he was still not over the loss of his true love.

Another goal I had in mind with this story was to show that he was not an invincible killing machine. He is one of the best in the business, partly due to the deal he struck with the devil, but he is still human and can make mistakes. In this story he gets captured, kicked around and while he did save the day, he didn't get the bad guy in the end. But there is a reason for that.

I like to call this storytelling method the Star Wars Parallel. You have a debut story with a definitive ending, yet open for the possibility of sequels (or prequels). Part two of the story, while it does resolve the matters at hand, ends with a sizeable cliffhanger, all but guaranteeing there will be a sequel. Heck, I guess Killdevil has a few things in common with Star Wars including damsels to rescue, evil family members, thrilling combat. Its just knives and tommy guns instead of lightsabers and blasters. But I digress.

To sum it up, I am quite happy with how this story turned out and still very much love writing the character. And while this may have taken quite a bit longer to finish due to one reason or another, you can rest assured that the Killdevil has not faded into the abyss of long forgotten pulp characters.

He has scores to settle and I have begun working on building his next epic chapter.

⊚⊚⊚

MARK ALLEN VANN - grew up in Northern Wisconsin, quite literally a stone's throw from the famous Lambeau Field, though his mind was always somewhere else: whisked away by the stories by Howard, Burroughs, Moorcock, and Verne. He would pursue interests in promoting heavy metal music, officiating roller derby, and several aborted attempts at writing a novel. Now he finally has a couple of books out and is picking up steam writing short stories in the great pulp tradition as well as running his own publishing company in *Xepico Press*. When his fingers are not flying around a keyboard, he can be found still in the shadows of Lambeau Field listening to music, watching wrestling or spending time with his family. You can find him on Facebook at the *Xepico Press* page.

THE ZIG-ZAG MAN

By Jarrett Mazza

WHEN THE BANK'S ALARM WAS TRIGGERED, he was already out the door.

Amidst crackling gunshots, relentless screams, the masked man zagged along the gleaming floor, gripping fat bags of cash while beaming with a smug confidence at those whom he moved past.

Giving a playful salute, it was followed by a coy, playful wink.

Who he was, they didn't know, but he knew, they would soon enough.

Across his eyes were two perfectly drawn zig-zags. On his body, a monochromatic purple costume with blends of neon red, and careful streaks of bedazzled jewels that ran along the chest, and around waist. Given his ability to cut, to rapidly change directions, what people witnessed when they did manage to catch a glimpse of such a captivating man, was a costumed individual who shined in the light; an aspect he took much pride in when compared to others.

You see me, then I'm gone. I'm the Zig-Zag Man who you will likely see zigging and zagging again.

A blaze of gunfire rattled above his head as he leapt over a table in the bank's spacious lobby. Falling down, he rolled along his arms, dodging more bullets that cratered the floor where he was once positioned. Pinned, yet by no means thwarted, The Zig Zag Man tumbled, and popped up behind a pillar while all the while maintaining his grinning visage.

"Close but then—*not close enough.*"

A playful taunt, what was a real thief if not someone who liked to poke fun at those who were quick but not too quick as to stand in their way?

Gawking at a squad of police officers, Arnold Zigler sprinted near the officer who was the closest to his position. Lightning quick, with reflexes that rivaled even the most ferocious cats that roamed the jungles, he snagged the gun straight out of the cop's hand.

"Gah!"

Burdened with shock, possibly with fear, once he had the weapon, Zigler pivoted, and knocked the cop straight to the floor. While his background in martial arts was scarce, and patchy in most areas, he did know a thing or two about takedowns as well as evasion.

Using a spinning kick once taught in karate, he delivered it well enough to knock the other officer down. Once done, he knew he had an opening, but was also left—*totally exposed*. Changing directions, his speed amplified, and he was running at full tilt towards the exit. Hopping, then cutting, his movements were a blend of synchronous juts, and swerves. When the cops at the bank weren't trying to shoot Zigler, he was hopping on tables, using the soles of his fitted boots to push high, and away.

Bending back, he twirled in mid-air, and yet, despite having a clear shot, none could nab the constantly moving, always shifting man that was impossible to get.

With the bags dangling from his arms, Zigler hid.

Not far from the door, there was only one way out of this crowded financial institution, and it was closed by the same people after him now. Cut off, with three squad cars parked outside—Zigler stood before the massive doorway, arms out, eyes down.

In the presence of a raging squad of uniformed officers marching right after him, he shifted again to cut across the doorway. Moving sporadically, Zigler's speed was immense, but his tactics were what was most impressive.

As he went left, every officer who made their way towards him removed their guns, *aimed*.

Firing through glass, all the windows shattered, and yet Zigler continued to push himself.

Flipping over while using the wall, he trotted up and twirled in mid-air. Dodging the other bullets while all the while managing to hold onto his two bags of cash, he rolled again, and raced towards the other side. Leaping through the broken window, he was posed in a classic jumping position; one leg extended out and the other locked securely behind him.

"Shoot!"

As the cops continued to try and peg the Zig-Zag Man any way they could, with each round spent, they missed him only by mere inches.

And inches—was all he needed.

Ducking, diving, dodging, when he was outside the bank, all that lay ahead were the patrol cars, and the street. Crowded, Zigler counted six officers in front of him now.

Catching his breath, he rarely—*if ever*—felt exasperated.

Able to control his breathing, regulate his heart rate, what was strenuous and difficult for some was that much easier for him. Not tiring, not even needing to take a second to recover, his ability to withstand pressure and to retain energy was a gift that not even he could explain.

Nevertheless, when he saw the other cops beginning to move in, his escape was far from over, and he knew he needed to keep moving for as long as he could.

Jumping over the hood of another car, he zagged once he landed, and piercing through the gathering of police, he was a rippling tide flowing around sunken stones. So close to their bodies, he blitzed, and once near enough to certain officers, Zigler cocked his arm, and delivered a bout of some extra pain.

Popping the men in their mouths, *he punched and then he kneed.*

Clobbering two in the gut, he pushed them both down, and using an old karate throw, locked one in the wrist, turned him down, and then flipped him forward. Listening to their hard exclaims, Zigler lifted the bag of money, and smacked another cop just as he was about to race off again.

"Shoot him!"

Hearing the voice of a man, Zigler ran in a straight line, and vacated the space with all the police cars, and headed straight for the dead center of the long road.

"Go! Go!"

Shuffling of footsteps, the reloading of their pitiful revolvers, part of him wanted to say that all the cops were merely crappy shots, but then he would be taking much away from himself if he were to admit this.

They weren't bad shots.

He was just too damn fast.

In the middle of the street, Zigler was in traffic, and in the presence of two approaching vehicles. Pivoting, then cutting, he split around the hood of the cars, rolled over, and escaped from more gunfire.

Hearing the bullets crackle and then burst, where he wanted to—needed to go—was not far now. A few feet away, lay the sewer grate, and past this, the tunnel which he would enter and finally put a close on his daring escape.

This close, this near to the last part of his daring evasion, and so—Zigler split.

Running as fast, as hard as his body would allow, it was not only about running as much as it was about *using* his speed to harness the full power of his surroundings.

Relying on the use of any neighboring objects, Zigler bounced off cars, telephone poles, flipping off fire hydrants, and rolling along the floor like a runaway tire to get to where he needed to go. While he had all these abilities, alas his body would have surely been compromised if he decided to do this. Without any choice, or any other *means* of moving, it was either this, or he fell at the hands of the squad of police officers who were now only just starting to close in.

"Shoot him!"

Hearing another officer's voice calling for his immediate death, Zigler ran towards two of the cops. With their arms outstretched, pistols aimed, The Zig-Zag Man leapt towards them. Splitting left, then right, he pushed off the hood of their car, and soaring high, he did a cartwheel in mid-air, and then fell down towards the back of their heads.

Landing smack behind them, Zigler kicked, and knocking one cop back, he used the push to whip his body in another direction again. Falling onto another car, he ran across the top of the vehicle, and reaching the other side, backflipped, he had now executed what would be his most difficult yet also his most necessary means of an escape.

Running, he zigged and he zagged, and whenever he approached a car or another cop, he'd jump up, hop over, flip back, *and roll*. Always in motion, not stopping once, the bullets cracked and exploded, and despite being close, not a single one managed to penetrate his wiry body.

None managed to land, and thus, not a single officer was capable of bringing him down.

Kicking another, when he evaded the fifth, it was to be his last.

In the middle of the street, he somersaulted once again, and fell back over the grate.

So close, he kicked the lid, and holding it up, *like a shield*, covered behind it.

"No! Don't let him get away!"

Hearing the yelling of the sergeant with bleeding face, he screamed as to rally the last of the officers together. While Zigler thought it was wise for them to spare their ammunition, and to waste not another bullet, they insisted on firing back.

Shooting him where he stood, the bullets pinged the metal, and ricocheted off the steel.

While the circular hulk of galvanized metal had considerable weight, Zigler didn't hope to hold onto it for too much longer. Soon as all the bullets stopped, he lowered himself back down, and flipping it forwards, gripped the edges like he was holding a frisbee.

Using his hips, he let it fly, and sent it flying towards the nearest officer.

Clobbering one in the chest, the man fell back, and then he lost his weapon.

Then, the space in the sewer, *was left wide open*.

"Stop him!"

Taking a second to admire his handy work, they couldn't catch him if he was so out in the open, which means in the sewer, they had zero chance of tracking him there either. Unable to see, and with a clear path to run straight, in full sprint, there was no one who could rival such speeds. And, with one bag still in his hand, Zigler let it go, and glimpsed back at the wounded, *defeated cops*.

"Bon voyage, gentlemen!" saluted Zigler. "It's been a real slice!"

Taking in the last of his escape, all the money robbed, and all the bullets dodged, soon as he fell into the tunnel, he was sure to be a goner. Slipping into the tunnel, Zigler landed smack down into the sewer. Hearing the shuffling of footsteps, the same orders shouted, and the same urgency placed while he was standing in a stream of muck, sewage, he raced and split down the long corridor.

Now he was gone.

A straight shot all the way to the end of the line, Zigler sprinted across the sewers, splashing his laced boots right into the murky water, and blitzing through the darkness without looking back. With both bags thankfully still filled to the brim, and gripping the knot, even with this much weight attached to his body, he still managed to maintain his speed.

While he assumed the police would pursue, because that's what they always did, he also knew that none would be able to catch him now.

Into the vast and expansive darkness, the highly trained, highly capable thief cackled in the shadows as he raced. Cut up and bruised, mostly, he had escaped relatively unscathed. Alive, and breathing, and with his body still intact, if he was going to go anywhere now, he would be heading to the only place he absolutely needed to go.

His boss and lord was a criminal mastermind known as No Face. Having suffered a chemical accident when he too decided to flee from police, he was doused with an acidic compound that boiled his face and scorched his flesh to the point where it melted off the bone. Refusing to wear a mask, his eyes, lips, and cheeks they had all merged together, and what was left was sprawling strip of white skin; with only two small slits left for eyes, and a mangled pair of neon red lips that barely moved when he spoke.

Now running almost all the crime in Spark City, the place Zigler called home, he was the one who hired Arnold to rob and to obtain valuable objects around the city. And, since there was only one Zig-Zag Man and no one out there who was good enough to catch him, God damn did he'd ever deliver. Running for almost fifteen minutes, going into the sewers was not a last-minute measure, but instead something that was planned, and calculated. Therefore, as Zigler moved in the vast space below, he stopped when he came to the grate that was outside of No Face's building.

Stepping up, he pushed it open, and lifting it out, fled from inside, bringing all the money with him. By now, his classic zig-zagged mask had peeled off his eyes, and only skids of the former shapes remained. While his identity was no longer secret, here, in the towering structure, the men employed were quite aware of *who* it was.

"Here to see the boss."

Stepping aside, two hulking men in suits, one lifted his hand, and gestured to the elevator.

Strolling on in, Zigler wasted no time, and headed straight to the top floor.

In the penthouse, a decorous and highfalutin office owned and operated by the city's most notorious criminal, sat a fat desk before an expansive window. And beyond the vast cityscape now aglow, sunlight engulfed No Face as he stood, and with a glare encasing him where he stood, and prevented Zigler from seeing him in full view.

Such was unnecessary, as Zigler knew quite well what he looked like, and preferred to skip over the part where he viewed him again.

"Boss," said No Face's chief bodyguard, *a man with long arms*, and slick hair who went by the name Colt. "He's here."

Walking across the gleaming floor, Zigler passed Colt as if he didn't know him, because the last encounter Zigler wanted at this point was a conversation with the help.

Here to deliver the money, that's all he was here to do.

"Yes," said No Face.

Due to the burns that at one point No Face had experienced, his throat was charred, and thus, his vocal cords, and voice were reduced to a raspy expulsion; *words that were barely audible to anyone who was standing too far away.*

"Bring him to me."

"No need," piped in Zigler, "already here."

Looking straight past Colt, he was a man whom Zigler had little time for.

Splitting from the doorway, he walked right out, but seeing No Face behind his desk, his mien was a mirage of appendages, nose, ears, and mouth, when Zigler was close enough to where the chief of all crime was standing, he plopped the bag of money down in front of him like he couldn't wait to let it go.

Hearing the coins clank and cash jumbled together in big, ethereal heaps, Zigler stepped back while No Face head turned down and he inspected.

"All here?"

"Every dime," answered The Zig Zag Man.

"*Hmm.*"

Once the bag was released, No Face opened it while Colt assisted.

Pulling the bag apart, from inside, big clumps spilled out, and No Face and his minion were suddenly both awash in cash and gold.

"Jesus—" said No Face. "You have really outdone yourself this time, haven't you?"

"Well, you know me," said Zigler, "I'm just in it for the name."

Hissing to laugh, while No Face could do little given his alterations, what he *could* do was laugh.

"That you are," he said. "That you are."

Nodding, Zigler took a step back, and gave his boss a modest, humbled expression.

"Indeed."

Snapping his fingers, No Face gestured to Colt.

"Well," he said, "give the man his share then, yeah?"

"Now?" said Colt.

Holding a bundle, Colt flipped the bills against his thumb and index, and was enamored by the sheer size of the score.

"Yes," ordered No Face.

While his eyes were concealed beneath a wrinkled line of scarred, grotesque layer of flesh, from the tiny slits, a harsh glower penetrated, and struck Colt as he stood by.

When No Face asked for things, whatever they were, he only asked for them once.

Moving away, Colt walked to a separate area and Zigler watched him as he did.

"You did well," said No Face, speaking to Zigler. "You did *very* well."

"Yes," he responded.

"And because of how well you did—I would like you to do it for me—*one last time.*"

Holding his gaze, Zigler's head turned from Colt, and he returned to staring at the staunch criminal lord who was his employer.

"*Again?*" said Zigler. "But you said this would—"

"Be the last?" said No Face. "Yes, I know I did."

"And?"

"And, well," he replied. "I changed my mind. However, this new project I have planned for you is—"

And before he could finish his thought, Colt snapped to, and was now directly beside Zigler, holding a leather bag that he then proceeded to drop down in front of Arnold like it was nothing.

"Worth your while."

"Another job?" said Zigler.

Now seated, with his hand jammed into a mound of cash, No Face's head peeled up, and he stared at Zigler; a look of sheer enchantment gleaming in place of a stern countenance.

"The last job."

Pausing for a second, Zigler considered the offer.

However, not wanting to show his frustration, part of his appeal as a thief was that there was so little that fazed him or disrupted his trajectory towards absolute victory. His ability to keep moving didn't just apply to his body, but to keep moving meant to continuously, relentlessly, concealing his true feelings towards the world that existed around him. Once he cared for something greater than himself, once he was a man far better, and deadlier than the one he was today. Used to be better, he was once a man who made an honest living, and yet, all this got him was a broken home and a world who never truly appreciated him.

It was only after this that he decided to become a thief.

While he proved to be sufficient at this, as well, what he could do, he did quite effectively. Working for No Face soon afterwards, he was all but a pawn in this great and terrible world of crime. However, when he was enough to please No Face, to satisfy the city's most dangerous criminal, then he was safe.

One job, one price—*one way out—*

"So—are you in or not?"

"One last job?"

"Precisely," said No Face.

Shrugging, The Zig Zag Man cared not for the money as much as he did about the primary question currently plaguing his mind.

What's in it for me?

"More secretive," said No Face. "Bigger, better than anything you've seen and done before."

"I see."

"I want you to take down a place called NewFound Capital, a fund that's

"So—are you in or not?"

currently using new technology to store its money and to trade with. No vaults, but instead they use these new digital—*hard drives* that carry sometimes hundreds of millions. A huge score, if you could go in, and do what you do best, I'll have my men help you with the drop off. All you have to do is find it, and run with it."

Shaking his head, Zigler scoffed.

"That much cash in one location—*impossible.*"

"That's because it's not in one location, you see?" said No Face. "Their security, like the way they store money, is cutting edge, and therefore—quite difficult to attain. Soon as you're in, you'll have an army of guards just waiting to get their hands around your neck, but then, when has an army of cops stopped you?'

The question posed by No Face was suitable.

And, given how many Zigler avoided today—it was fair to say that a squad of armed officers meant very little to him, whether it be fifty or seventy.

Such a stat made no difference to him.

"It hasn't."

"Exactly," replied No Face.

Growing irritated by what was turning out to be a platitudinous exchange, Zigler would be content to never hear from him ever again.

"Do this for me," said No Face to Zigler, *"and your debt will be paid."*

"Paid?" said Zigler.

Containing a cascade of flourishing feelings, mostly of relief and hope, he was embittered no more. Staying in an irritating conversation, he stared at his lord, and repeated back the words:

Debt.

Paid.

"Free?"

Posing the question now to No Face, once it was said, the brutal boss of all bosses, fell into his chair, and sat upright, nodding as he gazed.

The debt to which he was speaking of belonged to Zigler, who knew of this quite well.

Before he was The Zig Zag Man, he was once an athlete, one of the greatest, and then he was injured, and all that he had worked hard for—*all gone as if it never existed.* Of course, it didn't vanish solely because of an injury. When he was hurt, he thought he would never recover. Believing the best days to be behind him, he began to abandon what he once thought he would be forever loyal to. Turning to alcohol, narcotics such as painkillers and other sources of euphoric delights, he removed himself entirely from the life that once gave him so much happiness.

Once he fell off the cliff, and began to become overwhelmed by pain, and destruction, eventually his leg healed, and he was able to do what he once did. However, by then, the damage he had sustained as a result of his disconnection was completed.

Still endowed with a gift, he was unable to place it or use it in any capacity.

Gone.

However, it was only when he was at his lowest point that he came to encounter No Face and his minions of abandoned, broken souls. Doing as a great criminal was expected to do, he pulled Zigler from the debris, rebuilt him in the way that he said he wanted to be. Vowing to give him a new purpose, he also swore that should Zigler succeed while participating in this new game, once it was all done, *he would ensure his escape into a better life.* Promising to use all his contacts in the government, as well as the resources that a man like him had possessed, he swore Zigler could rebuild his life, maybe even reconnect and reconvene with the family that he had abandoned.

Saying he could do this, one day he hoped that he would, and while Zigler only gradually started to believe that such a day would never come—according to the man seated behind the desk—*it had now arrived.*

"Two more jobs," said No Face. "Two more banks, two more scores, and once the money is laid at my feet, I will raise my hands, and I will set you free. All you have to do—is say yes."

Taking a long, deep breath, Zigler gazed at the money that he had stolen.

Recalling how difficult and painful it was for him to recover, despite his talents, always he brought himself to the edge of oblivion—thinking there was no way out. He imagined doing it again, for anyone, under any circumstance—and this—this was what would happen to him if he accepted.

"I—I—"

Unsure about what to say—whether or not he would agree or pass on this idea—he didn't care about what was said or why; *when No Face made an offer,* there was only one way to answer him.

"I will."

A moment's pause, a time consider and to understand, not a word was said as Zigler stepped away from the desk; head down and ridden with shame.

"Good," said No Face. "*Very* good."

"Is there anything else you can tell me about this place you want me to enter and also destroy?"

"*Absolutely,*" said No Face, pulling the cigarette out of his mouth, he nibbled on the end, and then lit up before addressing Zigler through his gritted teeth.

Not knowing how any of this was possible, Zigler reflected on all the previous robberies that he completed for No Face; *the man whom he was staring at now.* To rob more banks would surely put his life at risk or, as Zigler was only starting to see, perhaps, seal his fate as one of the greatest thieves in history.

But to be freed from this life, to start over, was an opportunity that the legendary Zig-Zag Man had been waiting to receive for far too long. And, if this was the chance to acquire it, to own it, and to finally be let go, he knew he would have no choice.

"Colt will provide you with the details and you can start assembling your own methods for extraction. Once you have obtained everything you need, we will then arrange for a way to put you inside, and well then—then the rest is up to you."

"Unless—you got more questions," interceded Colt.

Glowering in his direction, Zigler had often made it clear that he was in fact the very last person he wanted to speak to.

"I see."

Closing his eyes, there was no time left for him to consider or re-consider, he already accepted the offer, and what's done—was done.

All that was left—*was for him to begin.*

"Ready?" asked Colt.

Looking back at No Face, still smoking his cigarette, smoke wafted in front of his face, and Zigler nodded, and then took a step back.

"*Yeah.*"

Having accepted, two days later, the location was selected, and the job was clear, and so, *Colt gave Zigler precisely what he needed to succeed in this upcoming mission.*

NewFound Capital.

Built with top-of-the-line security, there were guards, and there were also alarms, and extra safety protocols such as locking the banks down soon as they were being robbed. While Zigler could move, zip, and dodge almost anyone using a wide variety of acrobatics, his deep knowledge of gymnastics, and calisthenics, there were six guards total; all armed, and each one big and ready to shoot with their revolvers holstered.

The doors could be triggered with automatic locks and the fund was closer to the police station than the dozens of others Zigler had dipped his feet into. And yet, studying all points of egress and entry, Zigler spent a total of three days configuring the best methods for evasion.

How he would endure, and manage to escape under the most strenuous of circumstances, he couldn't imagine—

Nonetheless, he knew who he was, *and what he needed to do.*

Willing to run, cut, jump, and wiggle his way out of any obstacles, the more that there were, the more he was required to adapt. And yet, Zigler didn't care. He moved on to the next phase, and continued to examine the schematics laid out before him.

Unlike previous robberies, in this case, he had been informed by No Face that he would require help—*assistance*—and so, he brought in some of his own.

Along with Colt, there was another man who would be joining Zigler as well.

When thieving the last bank, upon exiting, he didn't have a mode of transportation as a means of escape. While running, he found access through the sewer, and he was going to be taken to the next place by an elite driver.

His name was Barry.

A hulking beast of a henchmen, he was recruited by No Face, and there was little that he decided to obtain. Focusing solely on his ability to find the ways in and out, Colt kept his eyes on Zigler the entire time and Zigler did the same to him.

"Do you know what's happening? Do you know what you're going to do?"

Colt, now the one asking questions, he was pretending to be no Face despite not having the status or the intellect.

He was a foot soldier, and nothing more—

"I *always* know what I'm going to do," said Zigler. "The problem is once the plan is in motion, you can't make it stop. You have to keep going—*until it's over.*"

"Well," said Colt, "I guess that's why they call you The Zig Zag Man, right?"

Pausing for a moment, he thought back to all the times whereby he was referred to in this way. He knew who he was, and knew what it is he liked.

Run, run, cut-cut-cut, zig, and zag, avoid and evade, he was both a liberator and an extractor, and he was someone who did whatever he needed to do in order to *escape.*

No matter what.

"The papers, they called me The Zig Zag Man," said Zigler. "It stuck, and I liked it, so—"

"So—you don't think that you are?"

"I think I'm a man who can get the job done," said Zigler, "and right now, that's all I want to be. Just the guy who can get things done."

"Well, you better hope you can this time around," said Colt.

Suddenly Zigler's hands clenched, and all the muscles in his fingers stiffened. Glaring back at Colt, why he said what he did, there was something strange, and ominous in the way he said it.

"What?"

Staring back, displaying a glower, his lips tightened along the bottom of his face.

He knew what he heard, *in the precise way he had.*

"What?" totted Colt. "This is your last job, so if you pull it off, you're out, but if you don't—"

Tilting his head to the side, he squinted, and moved away from the table where the map was located.

Hearing this threat, he knew what Colt was trying to communicate, and he didn't care.

"I don't—what?"

Grinning, *Colt eyed Zigler like the two were actually friends.*

While everything but friends, when Zigler inquired, the response provided became nothing more than a slap on the shoulder. Hitting him in the arm, he stepped past him, and then he made his way back to where he came from.

"Don't worry about it," said Colt. "Let's just keep planning, yeah? The job is two days away. It will be here before you know it."

Almost sarcastic, what Colt said, however, turned out to be quite true when the job that Zigler was in fact presented in an instant. Donning his usual purple and silver outfit, with two streaks drawn across his eyes, at nine in the morning, NewFound Capital was open.

In the car, with the Colt and Barry, Zigler stared at the doorway from the curb.

"Wait here," he said. "I'm going to get pass security, and then get upstairs to where No Face told me he's keeping the item he wants me to take. Hopefully, it won't take me long to gain access, but when I do, I'll grab it, and then—then I move."

Glaring at Colt, he nodded after Zigler explained how the plan was to be executed.

The inside of the car fell silent, and as Zigler gawked at Colt, then at Barry, the man in the front was quiet while waiting in the driver's seat. Without a word to say, Zigler was done dealing with the men who were only ordered to be present.

With nothing else to provide, Zigler latched his hand around the door, and walked on.

A statue of an important figure he could not name guarded the entrance. Seeing this, Zigler then took the most obvious hiding spot he could find. Concealed behind the effigy, he mimicked its pose, and was but a mime striking a position for what could be a very long period of time.

No one saw, *but then who was looking?*

Halting, he peeped in the space the arm and the head, and scoped out the door.

Emerging later from behind the statue, Zigler shuffled up to the door.

Careful, cautious, he scoped the entranceway.

With no one there, just him, he stared into the lobby.

A bustling complex, the place was comprised of mostly men sitting in individual cubicles, holding phones, barking loudly. So distracted by work, Zigler—*from farther away*—leered at the clean path that led directly to the top floor. Staring at what was a circular doorway, it was heavy, thick, and galvanized, *and as Zigler eyed the inside*, he also studied the guard who was poised next to it.

Only one, certainly Zigler had faced many more in the past, but the entire time, he reminded himself of what was going to happen when he made it through to the next level.

According to the intel acquired, the technology that guarded this bank was far superior than any other. Alarms, full lockdowns, the additional safety feature was one that not even he had seen before. Once the company sensed any kind of trespasser, a series of lasers formed into the shape of a grid, and thus, *prevented him from going anywhere.*

Standing in the doorway, he counted down.

"Ten."

Unleashing a heavy breath, he stepped forward.

Once through the door to the second level, he hopped along the rooftop lights—zipping on while everyone in the level below naively looked in the other direction.

Now up top, Zigler halted in between two elongated ridges; both inverted, and part of the décor. And yet, it was ideal for hiding. Surprised to see that no one actually saw him, when Zigler thought about just how often he did things so out in the open, he also remembered that people—generally—*were often so wrapped up in their day-to-day* that they noticed nothing except for what concerned them, and them alone.

The world is filled with obvious things, that no one by any chance ever observes.

Sherlock Holmes, one of Zigler's favourite characters in literature, coined the line that he did well to remember during his life.

Reading many of his books, it was always his intellect, his attention to detail, as well as his ability to track, and acquire which fueled Zigler and his interests. Trying to emanate him as much as possible, whenever he was pulling off a job, he always thought of the next step.

Using the ceiling, Zigler skipped using the lights as markers, and making as little noise as possible, zigged, zagged, and dodged until he reached the wall.

Glimpsing over his shoulder, then down—still no one noticed him.

Slipping out, he slid his body down to the ridge beneath.

Eyes up, *he looked at the lights.*

Holding his position, it was one hell of a leap he was about to do, and yet, he was ready to do it. Going ahead, he motioned to the left and then to the right—up and then down, and stretched out his leg, and in midair, flew across like an Olympic sprinter crossing a finish line.

Into the bank, he landed hard before he rolled.

Knowing that the next words would be for him to stop, Zigler headed straight for the second floor.

"Get him!"

Arriving exactly as expected, he neared the guard, jumped, and ejecting his foot—*socked the nearest guard in the mouth.* Hopping from light to light, too fast no one noticed, he cut from side to side, and flipped and landed gallantly before another armed guard.

"Hey, how you doin'? I'm The Zig Zag Man. Heard of me?"

Going straight for his sidearm, Zigler stepped to the side, and spun.

"Wouldn't do that if I were you?"

Pivoting, he missed the guard's head by mere inches.

Now behind him, Zigler placed his hands over his shoulders, squeezed, and then pulled him down to the floor. Rapid, succinct, The Zig Zag Man was a slick eel; impossible to get one hand on, and sometimes even damn impossible to see.

Hey, how you doin'? I'm The Zig Zag Man. Heard of me?"

With the guard down, Zigler pressed his foot into his throat.

"Why don't you just stay put, yeah?"

The guard's face was rubicund and his eyes were burning red.

He knew who he was, *and he was reading his warning loudly and clearly.*

No way around what was happening, for Zigler there was only one move left for him to make. With more working on the floor behind him, by now, they all knew what was about to happen. Although there was a robbery occurring right before their very eyes, and it was all so clear what was the next step.

Punching the guard clean in the face, the knockout was quick and effective.

Once he knocked the man out cold, he returned to his operation.

Moving to the higher level, Zigler saw that it was halfway opened.

Going on, he looked up, then across. Understanding there were new security protocols in place should someone attempt to trespass, while no alarm was triggered, what followed after was a series of additional obstacles that left him shaken—*cut off.*

Racing down through the second level, currently vacant, Zigler headed straight for the door. And yet, while he proceeded to the doorway, from out of nowhere—he was forced to come to a complete, *death-defying halt.*

"Oh—"

Speechless, and shaken, his hands were above his head, and he inhaled so deeply, it forced his stomach to curve.

From all around, a red laser grid formed that sliced straight through the lobby at a height of just three feet. When Zigler became caught in the web, he was fortunately now inside one of the squares rather than in the path of the red lines.

How this technology managed to manifest itself—he was without a clue.

Trapped in between the grid, Zigler was confined and, even for a talented escape artist, a squirmer such as himself, he found himself caught in the middle of something he'd never been in before. Guns aimed at the back of his head, Zigler loosened his arm muscles. With bags slumped to his side, and without anything to show for it, the mission would become a catastrophic failure.

But then so were his options, which were also becoming increasingly limited.

Head back, something pierced his sides, and then suddenly, he was exactly where he wanted to be, *needed* to be.

Assembling all his ideas, he surveyed the space.

With little room to move, the grid emitted scalding heat that was already starting to melt his costume. Nevertheless, his move was clear—go or get shot by the men who were now drawing in.

Shaking, he inhaled, and thinned his body best he could.

An already lanky fellow to begin with, it was his shape that enabled him to do some of the things he did, to achieve the feats that he had—

Falling to his knees, he commenced his escape from this mysterious grid. But, getting down so low to the floor, he performed the splits with long legs, and was then suddenly free from the perils of this security system. However, despite escaping a section of the digital net, he was now so low to the ground that the space that he had to move was immensely narrow. With his head mere inches from the lasers, strands of hair burned soon as he landed on the ground.

"Shit!"

Bending his body to the side, Zigler felt a deep strain in his ribcage, and then falling back, swiped his leg across. Now on his back, he was called The Zig Zag Man for the chief reason of being able to cut and change directions, as well as to use his environment as the main tactic for escape—what he was about to do next was not quite in his wheelhouse.

Still, now on the floor, and with his back nearing the surface, he rolled, kept rolling.

Then, flipping himself up, he began to dive. Contorting himself more and more, he bent while his body continuously in motion. Leaping into the squares between, he slipped in and out like he was in the middle of a highfalutin dance performance—each move perfectly aligned with a new tune. Weaving in and then out, Zigler hopped, and he flipped, and then he lunged in any direction he needed to without being zapped by the lasers. A near impossible task, it was the only way he could get towards the exit, which—the more he continued to perform such a mind-blowing task—the closer he came to the next door.

Performing a full back flip, he sent his body over the grid and used whatever momentum and space he had to dip and fall. Managing to slip out, once done, he raised his hand to salute. Although his miraculous abilities had spared his life, he felt like he was completely unable to do something like this again.

Jumping over stairs, he sprinted.

Jumping frantically over steps, he—The Zig Zag Man—skipped his way towards the roof.

Unable to slow, his slick costume doused in sweat, the fabric stuck to his body. Coming to the very top of the building, the roof itself was equipped with various prisms, ventilation grates, and other points of access.

And yet, The Zig Zag Man proceeded toward the center; specifically, to a triangular window that overlooked the marvelous, bustling floor below.

Looking down, so many standing around their desks, so few stopped to do anything.

An active setting and everyone there was either a customer or an employee.

No one in line, there were a few that seemed inattentive to anything except themselves. Certainly, a more challenging environment than used to, in this case, Zigler couldn't obtain the bags of cash as he did before.

No, unlike all his other previous robberies, what he needed now was attain something that was—supposedly—far more valuable.

In the instance of this operation, the man who oversaw Capital's trade was interested in a new endeavour now known as *digital currency*. While Zigler only had a vague understanding, most of the wealth that was either traded and shared, he knew it was not in a vault, like the last, but instead it was safeguarded in the hands of something worse, *a CEO*.

Bobby Timmins, a red-headed, suit-wearing individual, according to his profile, he enjoyed sneakers, power, and attention, a commodity he adored above all others. Wherever he went to in the space below, he was joined by people who showed him paper work and who consulted him with dozens of questions.

Of course, *all of this was observed by Zigler from down below.*

He didn't precisely know what they were asking him, but they did distract him, to a certain extent. Getting to Bobby, then finding whatever drive that contained vast sums of wealth, he couldn't be certain what or where it was at this time.

However, standing, and surveying the space below, Zigler refused to enter through the window like a foolish version of *Batman,* The Zig Zag Man motioned around the glass, headed towards the doorway, and then bouncing off the grates, used a pole to spin in mid-air, and fly with his legs first, and when he hit the ground, immediately he rolled.

All he needed to do was to get to Bobby, *get the drive,* and get out.

And yet, while he continuously played out the scenario in his head, *in his mind*, he was also insisting that it was far easier than it actually was. Bobby, hardly an intimidating men, what he had at his disposal rivaled anything Ziger had encountered in the past. Soon as he grasped what was to transpire, he would summon an army of armed guards and put an end to Zigler before he could even get six steps from the exit.

Although his skills could take him far, and they had, still they could not overcome logic of efficiency.

Able to zig, and zag, he could dodge and he could evade, and with his body hurting him immensely, and his muscles now so tender and weak, he was beginning to experience pain that he was not used to enduring.

Insisting he was still in tip top shape, he moved down the stairs, and approached a steel door twenty feet below. Pushing it gently with his shoulder, Zigler was struck by a cascade of new smells. Like rich cologne, complemented by an impressive scent of flowers, he knew then he was in the presence of class, and wealth.

Into the hallway, he began his trek across the long hallway.

Where he was now in comparison to the rest of the bank, right now—he couldn't determine.

However, he had no idea where he was going.

On the next level of the fund, on his way to Timmins' office, two shadows approached at the end of the hall, and he did his best to avoid being seen by the cameras, the ones that posted around each corner.

Able to do this by successfully bending his body, he leapt, and pressed his back into the wall.

Then, jumping to the ceiling, he was a spider sticking to the surface.

Hearing voices, and knowing they were coming closer, while the ceiling was suitable for a time, it was by no means the correct strategy for to be permanently concealed. Given the strength he possessed in his fingertips, being the Zig Zag Man who could cut and squirm through almost any space, when he was up, he could get to the ventilation grate—and he was so close to getting his hands on the metal grid, all he had to do was reach up.

No, when he inserted his fingers, he pulled, reached, and crawled.

Holding the grate with one hand and using the other to grip the edge, his leg went in first, and then he slid his body with his back in and across. Difficult, the control Zigler had over his body, always so immensely impressive, when he returned the grate to its original position, he turned over onto his stomach, and looked down at the two men passing by.

Laughing, they were two men in fine suits, and going on without looking up.

Zigler was thankful for this.

The next stop was to reach the office of the CEO, and from there have a conversation.

Rapidly crawling, again mimicking the properties of a scampering spider, he had the entire schematic of this building memorized. Knowing where to go, how far he had top crawl, he managed to control the hustling sounds produced as a result of moving at such haste, when he traveled for almost ten minutes, soon he found himself arriving precisely where he wanted to be.

Up high, he was outside Bobby Timmins' office, and gazing down below, he leered.

I see you.

Muttering to himself, soon he saw that he was not alone.

Another man was there with him, and they were speaking business, all of which The Zig Zag Man had little idea as to what the contents of their conversation entailed.

All he knew was he was waiting for it to be over, because he needed it to be.

Checking his watch, almost a full hour had passed since he vanished from the first bank, and the authorities were now collaborating and exchanging their own thoughts as to where he had ventured to. The Zig Zag Man was not only a *highly gifted thief,* he was known and hunted—and would continue to be hunted—every day of his life.

With the walls closing in, he could do nothing to stop it. What he wanted, was to infiltrate the decadent office of the man who had everything he required, sit him down, demand he give him what they both knew he was there for. While much had gone wrong since the completion of the first job, he recalled the words of No Face, the one who controlled his entire fate.

"I can give you your freedom."

Knowing this was the only reason he was doing this, now that he was so close to finishing it—*his patience ran thin.* As the men in Timmins' office began to depart, Zigler pushed the grate down, and slipped out of the long, narrow, *smelly* ventilation shaft.

Turned to face his desktop, Zigler slipped out, and crawled.

Still keeping himself high and out of sight, he went straight for the corner of the room, and posted up there like a bat caught inside, he made not a peep as he hid.

Watching other employees pass by, Bobby Timmins office was just a few more steps.

Waiting for the coast to be metaphorically clear, Zigler—using all the strength he had—pushed with his legs, did a full backflip, and then landed silently in front of the door.

Taking yet another deep, exasperated breath, he checked left to right once more just to be sure there was no one around.

From what he could see—*he seemed to be good.*

Stepping in, he heard Bobby Timmins voice. Sounding as though he was talking to someone, before Zigler arrived, he was almost certain he was alone. Seeing him now, sitting on a swivel office chair, Zigler stared at the impressive man who was worth far more money than one could ever hope to be worth. Nonetheless, once he was in, he looked at Bobby, who then looked right back at Zigler before he chose to speak again into his phone.

"I think I'm going to have to call you back."

Standing near the door, Zigler was patient as Bobby ended his call.

"Well, look who came to grace me with his presence, *the legendary Zig Zag Man,*"

Addressing Zigler with what sounded like genuine captivation, even still, he would have none of it.

"Lock the door. Stay still."

"What?" replied Bobby.

"I know you have an automatic lock, just as I know you have a silent alarm you are about to trigger. Do the first, not the second, and do it now."

"And you really think I'm doing to listen to you?"

"Yeah, I do," said Zigler.

"And what makes you say that?"

"Because if you know my name—then you know my reputation, and if you know that, then you know what I can do if you don't adhere to the warning I just gave. I can bend, curve, dodge, and *get out of the way.* While you're gifted in making money, talking to people, I walk a different path of ability, and I know you don't want to see which skills add up higher. Now, lock the door, and place both your hands back onto your desk."

As Timmins nodded, Zigler observed the inside of the room.

Looking for all multiple points of access, there was the door, another ventilation shaft—although he'd be damned if he ever went inside one of those again—and several windows. An incredibly large, and expansive window occupied the entire wall, and while it was big, it was not as high as Zigler anticipated.

Only about fifty feet, at least. When Timmins finished locking the door, he did as Zigler instructed. Both hands remained on his desk, and Zigler stepped in closer.

"So—if you're here now, then that means you must be here to—"

"Rob you?" said Zigler, close to the chair. "You could say that."

"I *did* say that."

"And now that you did, that leaves us with two options," Zigler explained. "You either give me what I want or you don't."

"Well, I gotta be honest with you," Bobby's demeanor was casual, *unimpressed*. He leaned forward onto the desk, and pressed his elbows into the surface. *"I really don't want to cooperate."*

"And I knew you would say that, but that's why I'm going to do things a *little* differently this time."

"Is that so?"

"It is. You see, instead of just taking the money and running away with it, I figured I would do what I never have, which is to just come right out, and ask for it."

"Ask for what, *exactly*?"

"May I have your money please—sir?"

Scoffing, Zigler's response could only be interpreted as a pitiful, and humorous attempt—also an outrightly asinine one—to get what he wanted. Despite this, Zigler leered and maintained his playful yet serious demeanor. Indeed, what he wanted to see transpire, what he was going to produce, even if it was a ridiculous, mind-bending thought.

"Sir?"

"Yes," said Zigler. "Like Oliver begging for his bowl of gruel. I would like some, please sir."

Grinning madly, the request continued to be met with mild amusement.

"You know," said Bobby, "with the snap of my two fingers, I could call in all the security I have into this room to take you down."

Sitting down, Zigler's stare narrowed. Looking into Bobby Timmins' fixated, watchful eyes, the threat given was not unexpected, but then he was not quite so inclined to take anything the wealthy man said seriously.

Truthfully, this army that he spoke of was not one that intimidated him, although the more time they spent speaking, the more time Zigler consequently lost.

"But then again," said Bobby, "you are the legendary Zig Zag Man, so I wonder if sending more people in here, would that even make much of a difference?"

"It wouldn't," said Zigler.

Now determined, he staunchly sat upright, and with his posture prim; he was professional. Hand on his lap, he presented himself not as a man in costume who was here to take money from a very powerful man, but rather as a client: someone who was here to conduct business and who was weighing his options in the presence of a man who could either accept or deny.

In this case, the outcome remained unclear.

"Well, then, I suppose to should just give you what you came for?"

"Now you're starting to get it," said Zigler.

As the smile spread across Bobby Timmins' unblemished face, his maddening visage only became more pervasive as he relished in the thought of surrendering vast sums of wealth all because the man who asked for it did so nicely, and *unapologetically.*

"I see," said Bobby. "And I take it that *Mr. No Face* is involved in this—somehow?"

"It's just No Face," replied Zigler, "and now, if you please—"

Standing up, Zigler extended his arm, and then opened his hand.

Like a spoiled-rotten child, he was waiting for the money he felt entitled to. However, having not yet fallen into his hand, still—he remained stoic, and continued to stand before Bobby Timmins without reservation or fear. A man so powerful and wealthy, Zigler's power, however, came from an entirely different space. While he was not rich, nor connected, he was the craftiest, most capable thief in the world. Bobby Timmins, who could deploy an army of security guards, he could also summon a brigade of cops, but to send such a force after such a man would only provoke him to use his own strengths against them.

Guns, bullets, the traditional methods of attack, all paled when compared to The Zig Zag Man's infamous ability to dip, duck, veer, cut, *dodge.*

Therefore, as of now, with Bobby Timmins cornered and confronted, Zigler knew that he was either going to hand over what he had—*or he would refuse.*

And *if* he refused, then Zigler would be forced to use the final arsenal in his vast skillset.

Rarely did he ever withdraw this one in particular, for most situations did not call for violence. And violence is used only when all other options have failed. If Bobby Timmins didn't hand the drive over to Zigler, then that was his choice, and that choice demanded one outcome.

"What *exactly* do you want?"

"The drive. The key to your new form of secret currency."

"I see."

"Your future."

"*My future?*" said Bobby, hand on chest.

"You're the one who created it, *this new way of storing and trading money—*"

"And that's what No Face is interested in, is he?"

Shrugging, to that—Zigler had so little to say.

"Don't know," he said. "Don't know. Don't care."

"You don't know and you don't care," said Bobby, curling his lips, and moving his head up and down, slowly.

Unimpressed with his answer, Zigler could see that he also knew the face of someone who was judging him quite well. And right now, *he was the one being judged*, and yet, unlike previous instances whereby someone would such on him, a thief, now—he did want to wear what Bobby Timmins had to say. A brilliant investor, money ruled every part of him, and if he wished to tell Zigler about how bad he was by spending his day taking from people, then he was all bloody ears.

Timmins, as Zigler knew, he took too.

He just did it in a way whereby other people didn't know they were being stolen from.

Even still, he did it, nonetheless.

"Who are you?"

And the question posed was not one that The Zig-Zag Man had expected to hear, especially when it was said with such intense stoicism. Certainly, he was aware that he was still being judged, but the tone displayed by Timmins made Zigler feel like he was being cross-examined.

"What?"

Fed up, running out of time, if this was going to be a lecture, then Zigler had no time for it. Rather pop Bobby in his head, take the drive, and jump out the window, if he were to do this, then there would be no surrendering the very thing he had come so far to get his hands on.

A bad plan, *he knew this well*.

Nevertheless, he also understood that Timmins wanted him to answer, or to think about how he was going to answer before he did.

Fortunately, Zigler already understood who he was.

"Who are you?" repeated Bobby. *"Who—are—you?"*

Speaking slower the second time, he spaced out his words so that Zigler heard each one clearly, and yet, he didn't require condescension or attitude. But, then again, he had come here to rob for someone, so perhaps the metaphorical ball was not in his metaphorical court.

He had no choice but to listen.

"I'm The Zig Zag Man."

"Yes," said Bobby, "and I know that's *how* you want other people to see *you*, but is that really who you are?"

"I'm the world's greatest thief. I can escape any situation," Zigler elaborated. "I move in and I move out, and I go, and no matter what, I don't—*I will not*—stop. With no end in sight for me, and so, I never plan for the future. I take, *and* I give, and I live a life of infinite directions, multiple ways of doing things, and I don't heed the advice of people who have lived lives with no meaning."

"And you think your life has meaning, do you?" asked Bobby.

"People know me, don't they?" said Zigler. "They know me, and so— they'll remember me."

"Yes, you are right. People—*will* remember. They will forever see you as a great thief, a man who was capable of so much, and yet whose name goes down with the rest of those who wanted something, but didn't have the will to obtain it the right way."

"There is *no* right way," Zigler, glowered at the self-righteous financier. "Not all good, not all bad—just the ones who weave in between, who zig, and who zag—*in between*."

"Is that what you tell yourself?"

And Zigler, silent again, this question—it hit deep.

There was so much that he, as a thief, tried to convince himself of. Sometimes it was that there were better days ahead. Other instances, he swore that there would come a time whereby he could finally quit this life and use his skills to achieve something far greater. He wanted this, then he was also aware that, so long as he remained fixed on maintaining his reputation, he would not be granted a life he'd only fantasized about. Nevertheless, the fact that it was raised here and now, only furthered his willingness to take what he was here for. Why Bobby Timmins thought he was seated on a higher moral base than Zigler shed more light on he, and others like him, saw themselves when compared to thieves.

While what they did was perfectly legal, their cunning nature, lack of empathy, as well as their total loyalty to the bottom line did not make them any better or more suitable. In Zigler's mind, he was in the presence of what was a new breed of thief: people who took from those who didn't know better and who were burdened by both naivety and ignorance, and with nothing there to protect them from the inevitable swindle and steal.

This was how these new investment organizations were making their money, and it was why no one held them accountable. With the emergence of this new digital form of currency—*technology*—places such as this could earn tenfold compared to what they did before, and what was happening now was only just the beginning.

"...forever see you as a great thief..."

Although Zigler was aware of this, as was Bobby, none of their knowledge mattered as much as who would walk away from this encounter. As of yet, Timmins had surrendered nothing and Zigler was, as of now, empty-handed. He had not robbed this man. All he had done for the past ten minutes was listen to a moral lecture about his name and his future. A speech that did force him to think and coerced a moment of introspection, Zigler shook his head, gawked, and insisted—

This was not what I was here to do.

Then, with his eyes up, lips coiled, his expression stern, he became imbued with an intense focus that turned his face rubicund, *compressed*.

"What I tell myself," replied Zigler. "Is I'm a man who can get things done. What I tell myself is I'm the best, and there's no one out there like me. There's no one faster, craftier, or more willing to do what it takes to deliver, because I'm him. I'm The Zig Zag Man."

Stopping there, Zigler stood with an outstretched arm, and then he opened his hand.

Done waiting, done listening, *done talking*, all that was left for him to do was to receive, and he was also done asking nicely.

"Give—it—to—*me*."

Nodding, Bobby Timmins sat back, smirking. Then, reaching into his drawer, without hesitation, removed the sleek, flat rectangular item that Zigler had ordered him to give.

Handing it to Zigler, the confident man did not resist nor did he look at all displeased to be giving it to the world's most capable thief. Instead, he was submitting it like it meant nothing to him at all. And, unsure how to interpret this unexpected gesture, Zigler didn't hesitate.

Snatching the drive from Timmins, what it contained—*he would not imagine*.

Pocketing it into his costume, he stepped back from the desk, slowly.

"But, of course, now that you have what you've come here for—" said Bobby, as he leaned back into his chair, "*time for me to get what I want out of this encounter too.*"

"And what's *that*?" said The Zig Zag Man.

"The chance to really see our classic Zig Zag Man in action."

Hearing his response, Zigler was aware that Timmins had the best security team that money can buy. He also had only just escaped a grid of lasers used as a countermeasure not long ago, and this was all a giant consequence when committing a robbery of this magnitude. And yet, so far— *Zigler heard no footsteps, no movements of any kind.* What he felt, however, starting to take shape behind him was a burly shadow that immediately cast a veil of darkness over everything that existed within the space.

"To face a single threat that even *he* is unprepared for."

"Wh—"

Before he could finish, Zigler was lambasted and was sent flying forwards into Bobby Timmins' desk. The sheer force that was mustered in order to push him was unlike anything Zigler had ever experienced.

Like being hit with a truck, so much power, and so much ferocity, he felt it in his entire body. Glancing up, he saw Bobby Timmins stand up from behind his desk, strolling around and going towards the door.

"Have fun," he said.

Watching him go, Zigler's face was puffy, rubicund.

With no air being pumped into his body, he couldn't breathe without taking a second to gather what little of his breath still inside, *and there was so little.*

He came face to face with a giant of a man standing at least six foot ten. He was a towering, bulky, and muscular man and he was as big as a truck. In the past, Zigler had faced men who were also big, tall, and strong. In this case, however, he wasn't looking at a man who was big, but someone far greater. While the word 'huge' was so often overused, it was indeed such a trite term, here and now, it couldn't be more accurate.

Having evaded guards, many were simple, but one was where things got complicated, especially when going head-to-head with a strong man in a closed space was where things got tricky. Few things to use to get away, not much to jump over, or to push off, the challenge with big men is they were slow, but powerful, and while Zigler was fast, he was also weak.

One solid hit from someone up close, and heavy he was certain to knock him down, and break him into pieces. Timmins left his office, and stepping out, the challenge of escaping only became that much darker.

Literally.

Stepping out, Bobby Timmins flicked on the light switch in his office and Zigler watched as the entire space turned pitch black. Unable to see his hand before his face, all he could hear in the shadows was the heavy breathing from the gargantuan man who was summoned to tear him to pieces.

Not an army of security, only one, and if Zigler couldn't see anything, then he damn well couldn't zig or zag, and if he couldn't zig or zag—he was as good as dead.

The massive window he once saw was covered by a row of thick curtains, and he hoped to see a hint of light somewhere—surrounded him was absolutely nothing besides infinite darkness.

"Uh—"

Moving in, the dark enshrouded Zigler, and while he was unsure how he was to navigate his way through the endless shadow, if he couldn't see, then how did this towering man manage to see him? More than this, *how did Timmins escape*, if he wasn't to be seen either? All of this did present certain challenges, and while he had the drive secured in his pocket, and acquired what he wanted, it was obvious now that the reason why Bobby Timmins gave him what he did was because he never expected him to escape.

Never been blind nor did he ever find himself in a situation such as this before, but fearing what would happen, Zigler tried to remember where the window was.

And yet, when everything looked the same as it was, he didn't know what was around him; in front of or behind. Everything was a continuous, never-ending wall of blackness, and if he wanted to step out of it, then he would need to go now.

"Ha-ha-ha—"

A cackling echoed from the hulking man who was there, judging from his callous reaction to the dim setting, Zigler could only assume that he could see. When he first saw him, his eyes were concealed by a pair of lenses that he thought were sunglasses, but evidently, like so much else he saw inside this fancy building, were a form of new technology that he couldn't—and might never—understand.

Why Zigler had *assumed* they were glasses, he loathed himself for thinking this—he couldn't help but feel a particular degree of hatred.

Too damn big, you should have done better than to get yourself trapped!

The drive stayed in his pocket and the first move that Zigler made was a careful, gentle step forward.

No sound made, fortunately, his ability to stay so light on his feet, was beneficial now.

Hearing heavy breaths, and additional movements, what he needed now was some light.

Ducking down, he lent his ear, and doing his best to organize the sounds to which he was hearing, and determine hulking man's position, he thought he was behind him, then in front, the breathing persisted, and his eyes popped to show captivation.

Feeling something inches from his chest, like he was standing in front of a closet, there was something there that was big, *unavoidable*, and he didn't need light to know just how close he was.

"I see—*you*."

From the dark, the hulking's man fist shot out like a cannon, and Zigler—although his hands were up—tried to deflect, but in a second, he was gone.

Falling back, hammering his desk, he rolled over it, and landed smack onto the carpet.

Before he could stand, the boot of the heavy man hammered him in his gut, which forced him up, and to fly into the nearest wall.

Hurting, his entire body felt as if he was being bumped full of fire, *acid*.

Throbbing, he took another breath, and tried to stand.

Pushing up while using his hands, five fat fingers enveloped his skull, and pulled him back down. Throwing him into the nearest wall, he pitched Zigler like a softball. Striking into the nearest bookshelf, he clattered, and using his environment, though he was prohibited from seeing, and not necessarily knowing what surrounded him—he knew the office, yes, and remembered the furniture, yes, and so, he knew where everything was, and so—this—*this was to be his light.*

Recalling it all purely from memory, he moved around, and leapt off the table, and exploded from beyond the darkness. Performing a flip, Zigler's might as well have had his eyes closed, all he was looking at now—*was black.*

Landing smackdown, he could feel the presence of the large man, but when he did, he made another move. Zigging and zagging, he zipped, and he rolled, and whenever this hulking man came close, he moved back again—

Rolling down, then back—Zigler pushed, and pushed, doing what he knew that he could. Jumping side-to-side, he could hear all the sighs of frustration from the man who was trying to get his hands on him. Going again and then again, he *could* still move, and when he did, he found a break that he could use.

The Zig Zag Man, more than just a thief, he was someone capable of getting himself out of any situation. He could jut, and he could change directions. Able to jump as if he were weightless, he was able to take risks that would surely cripple most.

He could do this, and he could also—*see*—

Moving like he was not blind, after enough sharp movements accomplished—he bolted beneath the man. With his large arms tried to grab at him, hold him, and pull him down—he jumped, and acting on instinct—*or as he saw it now*—faith—

Pushing off the desk, he soared towards a window.

Colliding into the glass, he was immediately struck with a wall of blinding light.

In mid-air, he looked back at the building to which he had once evaded, the face of the brooding man who tried to break him in two pieces, and then—then he was falling.

Descending, Zigler expected to crash into the pavement and flatten like a ball of dough.

And though he was prepared for this, in his hand, clutching it as it were a precious jewel, he held onto it, the precious drive that No Face had ordered him to recover.

He succeeded.

As he considered this—weighed his options—he understood the consequences, his descent to death was interrupted—

Landing on the top of the car to which brought him here, his back was hammered with hard, wet steel. Gasping as sharp spikes that had coursed through his body, he stiffened, closed his mouth, and then opened his eyes again. In pain, he couldn't breathe for a second and then he could—could because the fall didn't kill him.

It hurt, yes, but it did not kill him—

No—it *saved* him.

"Gah!"

Letting out a long, deep sigh, he was wide awake, and holding on.

"Drive!"

Colt, standing outside the front seat, looked up. Having shouted at the top of his lungs to move, *to go,* the vehicle bolted and vacated its spot by the curb. Blitzing down the narrow street, Zigler, with his body resting over top of the car, stared up at the building he had only just exploded out of, and watched as it—*all of it*—started to fade away.

In agony, the job No Face had ordered him to do was now complete. He had what he came for. Burning inside, Zigler did his best to channel his feelings of relief, and tried to bring it to the very forefront in order to alleviate whatever pain that he could. What was happening now he barely grasped, for soon he would surrender the money, and the drive that was secured in his pocket, and he would receive what he had longed for.

Freedom, *at long last.*

Resting on the car, Colt drove to a secret garage while Zigler continued to lay still.

"Help me."

Speaking to Barry, the two men moved around the vehicle, and pulled Zigler down.

Slipping him off, he landed on his feet. Dizzy, *bleeding*, he could not stand straight, and so, Colt pushed his shoulders in an attempt to improve his gait.

"You all right there?"

With eyes partially closed, Zigler dizzily turned, and looked at Colt, exasperated, and weary.

"Just take me to see him."

Refusing to waste any more time, Zigler trekked up the stairs, and headed to the room on the second floor. Into No Face's office, the section was equipped only with a desk, and nothing else.

"Zigler!"

Spreading his arms, shouting with rejoice and glee, the criminal lord was all but pleased to the see The Zig Zag Man returned.

"You are here and you have returned!"

Waiting in the doorway, Colt brushed past him, and went straight for the desk.

Lugging to his boss, Zigler's hand slipped, and he slid it towards his pocket.

Inspecting this section, the drive was still there.

"Wow," said No Face. "I must say you don't look good. Are you okay? Is he okay?"

"He leapt out a bloody window to escape."

"A *window*?"

"Aye, he landed on our car, he got what he needed, at least—I think he did."

"Jesus," replied No Face. "A window, *huh*? Well, I guess this last job asked a Hell out of you, did it?"

Not saying a word, the question was asinine.

No Face could see from Zigler's condition, and his state, it was obvious how much the job had hurt him.

"*You did it?*"

Captivated, No Face saw Zigler, but he hadn't seen the drive, and waiting for it to appear before him—Zigler pushed his hand as far into the pocket as it would go.

Seconds earlier, he felt it there.

Seconds earlier, it was there, *and now*—

"Do you have it?" asked No Face. "Do you have *that piece to our great puzzle?*"

"I—"

Hesitating, and Zigler never hesitated, he'd given it to No Face, yet, he asked him where it was.

"He doesn't—*I do.*"

Swinging his body around to face Colt, Zigler's neck cracked, and he felt his hand shake, before they dropped. Colt, No Face's so called right-hand man, was now standing back, flexing his chest. In his hand, appeared the drive, which he'd taken from No Face, and for what purpose—*Zigler did not know.*

So far Zigler knew, it was all going to the same person.

So far as he knew.

Seeing Colt's hand, Zigler gawked.

Although he now had possession of the drive, Zigler was without a single idea as to how he, Colt, had managed to acquire it, but he did, *somehow.*

"How did you get that?"

"Oh, I have my secrets too," replied Colt.

"So it would seem," said No Face, unimpressed, and coldly delivering his response with barely a fraction of visible emotion.

While Zigler was taken back by the gesture, No Face was completely intolerant of it.

Not his to take, certainly not his to hold onto now, soon as Zigler saw it, No Face stepped forward.

"I'll be taking it back now."

Grinning, Zigler looked at Colt.

Ignoring his boss's command, he looked only at the person who had stolen it.

"Actually," said Colt, wrapping his fingers tightly around the drive, "I think I'll be taking it now. Since this was the most valuable object you have ever been after, I'd say it's worth a shot trying to take it to someone else. You know how this game works. Always there's someone who's willing to pay more."

"What?"

Barely able to utter this word, a double cross was the last outcome Zigler expected or needed now.

"Is that how it's going to be?" said No Face.

"Don't act all surprised," said Colt. "You had me as your errand boy for too long. And everything you stole, whatever it was, it never went to us. You just kept it all for yourself."

Turning back to stare at No Face, Zigler found himself captivated by the accusation.

If all the money he stole wasn't shared, then No Face wasn't a good employer, but then Zigler had stolen a lot for him over the years, and he hadn't seen him use the money obtained for anything. In fact, now that Zigler had really come to think of it, he didn't recall No Face changing at all.

So then, he asked himself—*where did all this money go?*

"So now," said Colt, bringing the drive to his waist, "I'm going to take something back for *myself.*"

Lowering his right hand, with his left Colt pulled out a crisp revolver.

Appropriately, the weapon was actually a Colt.

"I see," said No Face.

Oddly calm in the presence of the stand-off, he made his way back towards his desk while Zigler stood by and watched as the confrontation unfolded in front of him.

"Well, it looks like I have made another *miscalculation* in my many business handlings."

"Yes," said Colt. "And it's one you can clearly not afford."

"Oh, I can afford it," replied No Face, standing tall, "believe me, because contrary to what you might think, I'm not in the thieving game—*never was.*"

A perplexed look soon began to show on Zigler's now wounded face, as it did for Colt, who continued to wield his gun. Claiming No Face wasn't in the thieving game was like claiming that Bobby Timmins—the one who Zigler had stolen the drive from—wasn't in the *making money game.* How he could say this after encouraging Zigler to steal for so long was all but mystifying, yet then again, *perhaps Zigler thought*, it was just a ploy to distract Colt from carrying out such a traitorous act.

"Sure, you weren't," said Colt. "Either way, I'm done serving, and now that I got this—who knows how much is on it, *and what it can grant me instead of you.*"

"Oh, I can tell you exactly what's on it," No Face insisted, "and I can assure you, it's not what you think it is."

Confused again, Zigler looked to No Face.

Behind his desk, still, he had not made a move.

"Yeah—"

Cocking his gun, Zigler stared at the henchman whom he despised, and waiting for him to pull the trigger, in doing so, knew that should No Face die, *then so would his freedom.* And, while he was in agony after his last escape, burning, and in need of medical attention, he wasn't going to stand by and let this garbage of a human being take from him what was rightfully his.

Having to act quickly, Zigler made a move against Colt.

At first, it was simple.

Picking up the object that was closest to him, he chucked it towards him, smacking him in the face, and then breaking his aim.

"Gah!"

Screaming, the gun fired, though it was not in the direction intended.

Aiming down, Zigler rolled along the floor, and springing up, stood before the Colt.

Now raising his hand, he attempted to shoot Zigler, and though he was right in front of him, and at point blank range, he zigged, and he zagged, and dodging gunshots, had a little fun with the man who thought he was better than he was.

Enjoying the back and forth, *despite his injuries*, Zigler accomplished what he wanted.

Still endowed with this gift of squirming his way out of any situation, even ones so up close and personal, once the weapon dropped, he ended it once and for all. Clobbering Colt with a straight elbow to the chin, he popped him clean in his face. Then, with both arms extended, pushed him right down like he was nothing but a mannequin standing in his way.

Seeing it drop, Colt landed flat on his ass.

However, with the gun still in his hand, he tried lifting it. Zigler, who was prepared to do as he did before, in the midst of pivoting to the left, then to the right, another shot was fired—*taking him off guard.*

A smoking barrel, silence followed shortly after.

Colt attempted to shoot Zigler and No Face, wielding his classic Smith and Wesson, until now Zigler, nor anyone, had seen him fire a weapon.

A first time for everything, Zigler noted, today it was aimed for more ways than just one.

"You really can't trust anyone in this business, can you?"

When No face uttered this rhetorical question, Zigler was fully prepared to answer, except the way in which it was spoken was more surprising than the shot itself. With a different voice, it was clear, resolute, *it was said as if the man with no face, and no lips, suddenly acquired all of the facets one would require for sounding as lucid as they had.*

Squinting his left eye, Zigler leered at No Face, and in an instant, felt his heart sink as but another deathly—*Earth shattering*—revelation was then presented to him.

Holding the base of his "face", his hand slipped up to his forehead.

Dragging a patch of skin up and across, his once mushed, and misshapen visage was lifted, and from underneath—the face of a new stranger; *a new face.*

"I know," he said to Zigler, holding up his hand. "Surprising, *yes.*"

"You're—"

Pointing with his right hand, Zigler stood by, and so hyper-focused, his hand quaked and practically uncontrollable. Beneath the former demeanor was the face of a man no older than forty, with olive skin, clean teeth, and a thick, flowing head of hair.

Handsome, far more handsome than Zigler himself, his mind continued to spin as he assembled all the ideas that were now piling up inside his head.

The first, and only one that needed answering was how—

How was any of this—possible?

Who was this man standing in front of him?

"I *have* a face," replied the man once known as No Face. "And no, I'm not the criminal you thought I was."

Gazing ahead, Zigler lowered his hand and tried to think of an exit.

If he was wrong about No Face's identity than he was potentially wrong about so much more, including and especially the man's intentions. Giving him work, *jobs*, the last of which he swore that once he completed it—he said he would be granted freedom, if that was *still* on the table? Or was he, Arnold Zigler aka The Zig Zag Man merely a pawn in a greater, now unfolding game?

"You can certainly say that again."

A new voice emerged from the back of the room and Zigler turned, and then he jumped to take a look. Not someone who did this easily, it took much to give the world's greatest thief the willies, but given the circumstances—*what he'd seen and witnessed*—his lack of stability was justifiable.

Truly, *he had no idea.*

The one who spoke was no stranger. And yet, the fact that he was familiar, only deepened the crippling levels of confusion that Zigler was currently experiencing.

Bobby Timmins, the owner of NewFound Capital, the company to which Zigler had recently stolen from, was now in No Face's office. Strolling into the scene, he was cordial, even chummy, upon arrival. Pointing at "No Face", Timmins sauntered, and moving right past Zigler, it was as if providing an explanation was something he was currently unwilling to give.

Or perhaps, Zigler questioned, *he didn't feel as if he was owed one.*

Strange, *however*, he felt completely different.

He didn't just feel he was owed an answer, he felt like if he didn't receive on in the next few seconds, his mind would bend and his sanity would vanish. Part of him believed he was hallucinating everything seen thus far, and then he heard "No Face's" voice once again.

"You look confused, and I can certainly understand why."

Grinning, Bobby Timmins stood with No Face, and both looked back at Zigler, nonchalant and casual as his former "boss" raised his hand to gesticulate to himself.

"As you can see, I'm not who you thought I was, am I?"

"And as you also see," interceded Bobby Timmins. "I'm not *either.*"

"What the hell is happening?"

Looking around the room, a lost child in search of his parents, Zigler was reduced to someone he never was as his mind was circled the same as his body.

"What's happening is—a test," replied "No Face".

"*A big test,*" continued Timmins.

"The biggest test you have ever taken, in fact," "No Face" continued. "And my name—it's *not* No Face. Never a good name begin with, I know, but it was the best alias I could come up with at the time."

"*Alias?*"

A loss for words again, the less Zigler saw the situation as sensical, the less confusing it became, although the level of confusion to which he was experiencing was still quite burdening.

"My name is Special Agent Frank Marshall."

"Although, I'm *still* Bobby Timmins."

"I work for a new branch in the CIA," said Marshall, former criminal known as No Face.

"We call ourselves G-Men."

"You're spies," said Zigler, speaking Timmins.

"*He is,*" Timmins pointed out. "I'm just—well, let's just say—I'm the guy who gets things for the guys who are spies."

"And you're the guy," said Marshall, speaking to Zigler only, "who can get *out* of things. Ever since I hired you, I—*we*—have been tracking a new criminal enterprise now growing in Mexico. We need someone who can get us intelligence on them, someone who is, for lack of a better word, *not* a solely a criminal, but someone with skills and prowess like yours who can beat the bad guys at their own game, someone with—"

"*Guts,*" finished Timmins.

"We have been watching for a long time, Zigler, and when I found you, I needed a way to get to you, so—"

"So, you disguised yourself as a criminal, and moved up the chain all to get me to pass your silly test?"

"*Silly?*" said Marshall. "You have no idea what's at stake. New criminals are rising every day. We needed to see what you were capable of."

"Or more importantly," said Timmins, "what you were *willing* to do."

Returning to that dark room whereby he was taking on Timmins' massive bodyguard, what he was willing to do was anything.

Zigler figured that they already knew this.

"And by putting you in a nearly impossible situation, did we come to see that you, The Zig Zag Man, did live up to his reputation. You were everything you said you were," said Marshall.

"And *more.*"

Timmins, who continued to finish his partner's thoughts, Zigler still wasn't sure if that was in fact what he was, but for some reason the need to finish bordered on the idea of making him seem stronger. And the fact that they could jive together only further proved that the two were very much on the same page.

"And that's why—*we want you.*"

"I thought you said I was *free.*"

"You are," said Marshall. "Or at least—*you will be.*"

"All your criminal records will be wiped clean, and you will have that fresh start you've always wanted," said Timmins. "The only difference is you'll now be on the right side, and you won't be wiggling your way as you flee with money—"

"You'll be stealing secrets, the kind that just might change people's lives."

"Maybe—even *save* them."

Marshall and Timmins, playing off each other like a pair of talk show comedians, they were so in tune that they finished each other's sentences. Then—circling around Zigler to put a bow on their sales pitch—his entire life was when whereby he had become a thief.

Considering that he might have the chance to be something more, maybe evolve and escalate into a more impressive specimen; his goal in life was always progression, never status.

"Chance to be a hero, *make the Zig Zag Man someone people can believe in.*"

"Believe in?"

Holding this blissful, gratifying thought in his mind, Zigler was never believed in or admired. Running, he acquired, he jumped, and then he kept moving. And yet, he was set to jump again, only before him now was not a building or the ledge of a steep drop.

On the contrary, it was a choice; *a leap of faith.*

Looking at his hands, broken and bruised, there was blood, and the wounds he sustained were still very much there, and thus, still throbbing.

"Something more," said Marshall.

Closing his eyes, meditating for a moment, he knew now there was no freedom without purpose, and his had just changed.

"Interested, Zigler?"

A courteous smirk, a blink of an eye, Zigler grinned.

"*I am The Zig Zag Man.*"

THE END

WHO IS THE ZIG-ZAG MAN?

When Ron Fortier offered me the incredible opportunity, that is to write pulp fiction for his amazing company *Airship 27*, my mind was a whirlwind of new thoughts and tantalizing ideas. Heroes from the 1950s, a legendary time in fanboy fiction, villains from the pages of those old crinkled comics that I love so much, and the kind of pull-him-off-the-rack stories that were once a staple of American (and Canadian!) popular culture, didn't just tickle my fancy, it provoked it to the point where it massaged my consciousness in a way so few things do.

A fan of pulp ever since I was a child, and now a self-proclaimed Grindhouse cinema aficionado, a living, living, breathing by-product of the 90s—both in terms of movies, television, and old-school kick ass action heroes—I couldn't tell you how many times I rented *The Phantom* or *The Shadow* on VHS as a kid; two properties I still consider myself a fan of to this day.

Producing a deep, resounding effect on me, as all of it did, now I desired nothing more than the chance to be a part of a community that adored these characters as much as I did, and fortunately, a community such as that does exist, and I'm happy to say that I'm now a part of it.

So, where did this idea come from?

How exactly did *The Zig-Zag Man* emerge?

Was it childhood nostalgia?

Was it due to the immense digestion of superhero fiction consumed on a daily basis or was it plainly from the will to write and wanting to impress Ron and his sect of loyal excited readers? To be perfectly honest, I don't really know where the origins of such a character had come from. However, when Ron said I was free to create my own, only then did I truly start to think about all the possibilities, both familiar and unfamiliar at the time. Thinking about the best way to formulate said character, I thought about the typical ones that came with the long list provided to me by Ron at the inception of this long, glorious saga. Liking *The Purple Scar* and *The Green Ghost*, the idea of renegade thieves, of all the characters I created, none of which were robbers, thieves, or men who took part in heists, but then this would be entirely unchartered territory, and approaching the unknown—for most writers—might seem counter-intuitive, intimidating, or downright a no-go.

For me, however, I had but one thought.

Let's go!

Considering the influences of the characters that I listed, I added a touch of *The Riddler*, a fanatical supervillain with whom I have the utmost affection, it was all seeming like it was coming together rather nicely. Thinking up some names in the process, whenever one tries to find one for a hero or a villain is a tumultuous task, that is given the plethora of others out there.

So, I thought more.

What can he do?

What's going to make him interesting, but also different?

Truthfully, I was fan of parkour and circus performers for a long time—envious of the people who can move and contort their bodies in such a way that is once thought to be almost impossible. And, with enough thieves who are already hackers, experts, safe crackers, I wondered, what if there was someone out there who was *neither*? What if there was a character who could simply walk into the banks, and then using his body, his athleticism to avoid, dodge, contort—zig—and—zig—*his way out of the many obstacles he was going to face*? A stretch—pun intended—it was something that hadn't been as explored as the others, so I figured: pulp, new, original, something that was both amusing as well as original, sure—*this could work*.

With pen to paper or, in this case, finger to key, I began writing.

Thinking of where I was going to put this *Zig-Zag Man* that I had conjured from the perilous sections of my blissful, boyish memories, what I was going to do to him, how I was going to challenge him, and what forces he could endure or overcome, the ideas for this simply kept flowing. Taking shape gradually over time, he was, in the end, a definite streamline from the characters I had sought for inspiration. A story that had taken me two months to actually shape, and another one to edit, eventually, I had a story that didn't just fit in nicely with *Airship 27*, but also something that would make Ron and his readers gleeful, if not completely entranced.

Wishful thinking, indeed, this is my first story after being welcomed into this new group of fanboys just as daring and foolish as I am. Always reticent about how the first one might playout, however, if there was but one lesson learned from this amazing experience, it's when it comes to pulp fiction, the stories I have will never truly end, and there's always another one to let out, tackle, and bring to light.

This is where I want to be, what I was bred to do, and I look forward to the road ahead.

I'm ready, I hope you are too.

Let's begin!

JARRET MAZZA - is a graduate of Goddard College's MFA in Creative Writing Program in Plainfield, Vermont as well as The Humber School For Writers. Before completing his terminal degree, Jarrett studied writing at the University of Toronto School of Continuing Studies and comic book writing under Ty Templeton and Andy Schmidt. He has had stories published online in the *GNU Journal, Bewildering Stories, Trembling With Fear, Aphelion, The Scarlet Leaf Review,* and *Toronto Prose Mill, The Fictional Cafe.* His work is featured in anthologies by *Silver Empire Publishing,* a best seller, *Zimbell House Publishing, NBH Publishing, MuseWrite Press,* and twice by *Dragon Soul Press, Gypsum Soul Press,* and *Hellbound Books.* All are available on Amazon for purchase. He was also an Honorable Mention for the Freda Waldon Award for Fiction, nominated for an Indie Book award, and was featured as a visiting author for the nationwide We Read Canadian event in 2020. He lives in Hamilton, Ontario.

You can follow him on Twitter @JarrettMazza (jarrett.mazza16@gmail.com) (jarrettmazzawriter.com)

www.ingramcontent.com/pod-product-compliance
Lightning Source LLC
Chambersburg PA
CBHW051136260626
47170CB00005B/1840